Birdie's Book

The Fairy Godmother Academy

BOOK 1

Birdie's Book

Jan Bozarth

decorations by Andrea Burden

Random House 🏠 New York

Visit us on the Web! www.randomhouse.com/kids

Educators and librarians, for a variety of teaching tools,
visit us at www.randomhouse.com/teachers

Visit www.fairygodmotheracademy.com

Library of Congress Cataloging-in-Publication Data
Bozarth, Jan.
Birdie's book / Jan Bozarth. — 1st ed.
p. cm. — (Fairy Godmother Academy ; 1)
Summary: When twelve-year-old Birdie goes to meet her grandmother, who is
estranged from Birdie's mother, she learns a secret which leads to fantastic adventures,
new understanding, and a renewed closeness among members of her family.
ISBN 978-0-375-85181-0 (trade)
ISBN 978-0-375-95181-7 (lib. bdg.) — ISBN 978-0-375-89290-5 (e-book)
[1. Fairy godmothers—Fiction. 2. Fairies—Fiction. 3. Grandmothers—Fiction.
4. Botany—Fiction. 5. Family—Fiction.] I. Title.
PZ7.B6974Bi 2009
[Fic]—dc22
2008036258

Printed in the United States of America
10 9 8 7 6 5 4 3 2 1
First Edition

For my grandchildren: Bella, Kailey, and Kirian

Contents

Part One

Seeds

1

The Long-Lost Grandmother

The train sped along, the wheels on the tracks whispering a humming rhythm . . . *Shh-shh, shh-shh, shh-shh, shh-shh* . . . as if they were telling all of us passengers to *go to sleep, go to sleep.* But I didn't want to fall asleep, because it was my first time on that train from New York to New Jersey. It was also going to be the first time I would ever meet my grandmother—my mom's mom.

It was New Year's week, and when Mom was called off to London, I had a dream that I met the grandmother I'd only heard about and who was now so close by. My father had always liked my grandmother, and he was sad that something had happened between her and Mom. Having lost his own mother, he was all for enjoying family while they were alive and kicking. Still, Dad had always told me that he respected my mom's privacy on a very sensitive issue.

That's why I was totally surprised when my dad had said yes when I asked him if I could go. But he said that it was high time for this feud to be over, and what better way to end it than by holding out an olive branch (that would be me) — even if the wrong person was holding the branch (that would be him). Dad added that this was the perfect chance for me to go meet my grandmother, just her and me, for a few days, and that he would talk to my mom and take full responsibility. He actually seemed to be looking forward to it!

"I'd come, but I'd just be in the way," said Dad. "Like a second fiddle. And just between you and me, I don't think Mo has got an ounce of craziness in her veins. And I know she's dying to meet you." My dad always called my grandmother by her nickname, Mo, and it's what I always called her in my mind.

So that's how I ended up on the train. Now, in between the anticipation and the train's lullaby, I had a jitter in my stomach, jumping like a bug on a leaf.

Shh-shh, shh-shh . . . Shh-shh, shh-shh . . . Bump! My head hit the window, waking me with a jolt. I'd fallen asleep after all. I looked down to check on my daisy, Belle, and saw that somehow her little clay pot had cracked.

Oh, I almost forgot somebody is reading this. I'm nobody special, just Sarah Cramer Bright (nicknamed Birdie), from California (which I like to call Califa). But I'm not from Califa anymore, I guess, because over Christmas I was painfully uprooted and moved to New York City.

But maybe I'm getting too personal. So before I go on, I must ask you to do something important: Please, please, *please* promise me that you will keep everything I say private. I don't like telling people really deep stuff about myself that is absolutely, positively not for public use. So please don't share this with anybody else, except maybe your very best, most trusted friend, okay? Because I guarantee you—not everyone will understand.

So, assuming we have a privacy pact, I'll tell you again that I am Sarah Cramer Bright, nicknamed Birdie by my dad (in honor of my red hair, which reminds him of his favorite California redbird). My mom says that my red hair and green eyes have been passed down from my great-great-grandmother Dora, who was Irish. I am told that my eyes twinkle bright emerald when I'm excited, but turn to dead moss green when I'm worried.

I took my feet off the suitcase that has been in my mom's family for years. My mom had specifically instructed me *not* to bring it. She always insisted on far more upscale luggage, like the matched Louis Vuitton set that she took with her to London the day before I left. There are people in my mom's world who actually judge her based on the quality and quantity of her bags! Not people I'd choose to be around!

Since my own trip was just a three-day jaunt to my grandmother's, the only other thing I brought was Belle, now in her sadly cracked pot. But I'd be at my grandmother's soon, and from what I'd heard from my dad, she would certainly have a pot for me to put Belle in. Dad had said that she was pretty much a botanist, rather like Luther Burbank, who grafted plants to make beautiful new species. I took my hat off and carefully tucked Belle into it, cracked pot and all.

The train door opened—crank, *swish*. I dragged my bag behind me, ba*BUM* ba*BUM* down the steps. The second my feet hit the platform, my face was slammed with little bits of ice, and my hair whipped wildly around in the wind. My braces were actually (truly and actually!) frozen to my lips.

I set the suitcase down on the platform and put Belle on the ground between my feet. I quickly zipped my spring green corduroy jacket to cover my favorite T-shirt and pulled on my gloves. I was not much warmer. I loved the jacket, but at that moment I realized I had not been very practical when I left this morning. I sighed. I guess my mind had been in Califa when I packed.

I picked Belle up again as the train rushed away. Around me the conversations mixed together in a rising mist that matched the overcast skies. I saw no sign of the grandmother I knew only from mailed cards, homemade gifts, my dad's few and careful descriptions, and my mother's stories about the "crazy old bat" who raised her.

People hurried toward warm cars with lightly purring engines, and I sat on my suitcase to wait, cradling Belle in one arm. Then I saw an older woman in a cowboy hat with a peacock feather striding through the drab crowd in the parking lot.

It *had* to be Mo. She was very tall and was smiling a big smile. Her boots must have been leaving size-nine imprints in the snow. As she came closer, I saw that her long green wool coat, as bright as spring leaves, was the exact same color as my own jacket.

Around her neck was an orange scarf with black specks.

I had a new name for her immediately: *Lilium tigrinum*, the Latin name for tiger lily, a constant tropical bloomer. That's practically the opposite of Mom, who is more like a calla lily (*Zantedeschia aethiopica*) — straight and stiff and stoically beautiful. Naming people after flowers and plants is one of my games. It's a great way to pass boring hours at school. Of course, I never use the same name twice, not even for twins. I know a lot of flower names!

"Birdie!" the woman said with certainty.

"Grandmother Mo *Lilium tigrinum*," I wanted to say back. But instead, I said, "Uh-huh," and clutched Belle a tiny bit closer.

Mo's voice was similar to Mom's but happier and, surprisingly, younger-sounding. Her hair, which curled out from under the hat, looked like it was mostly gray but maybe had once been red like mine. Her face? Smiling and kind, with lines creased around her eyes and the corners of her mouth. Not a trace of makeup. Her clear green eyes studied me matter-of-factly. I matter-of-factly studied her back. This was *not* the face of a crazy old bat.

"Well, well, Birdie Cramer Bright, I wouldn't mistake you for anyone else." She wrapped me in a tight hug that blocked the chill of the blowing wind.

"And you're wearing the family color," she added, patting the sleeve of my jacket. "I'd say I'm finally a working grandmother, and it's about time! Hallelujah for your dad."

"Okay" was all I managed to say, all of a sudden wondering what I was supposed to call her. Can you tell that I'm not good at first encounters? I like to size up a situation before I start giving anyone a reason to judge me or to not like me or to think that they like me when in fact they don't know much about me at all. Does that make sense?

We fought the wind as we walked to my grandmother's yellow car. Mo had to hold on to her hat to keep it from flying away. The car was as huge as a boat and had fins like a fish. I loaded my suitcase in the trunk and then settled inside on the wide front bench seat, my daisy-in-a-hat on my lap.

As Mo drove (I couldn't stop thinking of her as Mo!), I imagined that the big-finned boat-car was swimming along over the slick roads. Inside, the car smelled like leather and gasoline, and the heater warmed my hands and Belle's roots. The engine surged as my grandmother navigated an icy hill on the way to Colts Ridge, the town where she lives.

Halfway through the quiet drive, Mo glanced

sideways at me. "Quite a difference from California, I guess?" she said.

"Yeah," I said, nodding.

"I can tell you miss it," she said.

"Yeah, I do."

"And this will be your first New Year's in the snow, I suppose," she said.

I nodded. I could not find anything positive to say in response to *that* sorry fact.

"From what your dad says, your mom finally landed her dream job and you had to move to New York. Then, boom, they send her clear to London for that big paper account. But there are upsides, right? First of all, you're in *my* neck of the woods, so hopefully we'll see each other more often. And . . . aren't you looking forward to starting at that international school?"

The hand not holding Belle went straight to my mouth, covering my braces. As if thinking about a new school wasn't bad enough, I still had the brand-new stupid braces to make it worse! "Yeah, I guess," I said. I wasn't at all sure. I knew I'd meet girls from all over the world there, so it might be cool at the Girls' International School of Manhattan. Then again, starting school midyear isn't something you'd call easy.

Lilium tigrinum was not looking at me or at my
es. She had her eyes glued to the road. The
wipers slap-slapped the windshield as she tapped the
large steering wheel with her thumbs. "Well, it was
definitely high time you visited your grandmother,
dontcha think? The last time I saw you in the flesh
you were squiggling around in your mom's arms."

I knew I should have a snappy, cheerful response to her chitchat, but I couldn't think of one, so
I just gave a sort of snort.

"I've been thinking." My grandmother tried
again. "How about calling me Granny Mo? Mo is
short for Maureen, and no one else in this whole
world calls me Granny. Or do you prefer Grandma
Mo? Nana Mo?"

I was afraid she'd keep trying to find the right
name, so I said, "I don't know," and I turned to gaze
out the window at the passing mounds of snow.

Mo fell silent. I was afraid that I'd hurt her feelings, which I didn't want to do. It's just that . . . well,
I was already liking my grandmother a hundred
times better than I had imagined, so much better than
I thought my mom would ever want me to. It felt
weirdly like a betrayal to Mom. And if I acted like I
liked my grandmother right now, and *then* she turned
out to be a crazy old bat after all, I'd be in trouble.

"I think I'd like to wait till we . . ." I paused, trying to think of the right words.

"Till we bond?" she asked. She nodded, like it was a decision not to be taken lightly. "Sure. And just Mo is fine, too, if that feels better. It's what most people call me." Mo flicked on her turn signal. "What's your flower's name?"

"You think I have a name for a plant?" I asked, keeping my tone neutral.

"Of course!" said Mo. "I know *I* would."

Tiny snowflakes swirled past the big windshield, dancing on the butter yellow hood of the big car. Mo turned on the wipers again.

"Belle," I said, smiling a little.

"Ah. Short for *Bellis simplex*, no?"

Hmmm. She *did* get it. "Absolutely," I told her, my tiny smile expanding, but not enough to show my braces. I drew in a breath of the warm heater air. It was the first deep breath I'd taken since I got off the train.

"We're here!" Mo announced, turning the car slowly onto a snowy drive that wound between two trees standing like bare-leafed sentries.

"They're sugar maples," said Mo, nodding to the two trees. "My own mother planted them for me, fifty-some-odd years ago. Grand, aren't they?"

"*Acer saccharum,*" I murmured.

Now it was Mo's turn to smile. "Speaking of *acer*s," she said as we continued down the driveway, lined all the way with two rows of smaller trees, "I planted all these moosewoods for *your* mom, right after she was born."

Did Mom even care? I wondered. I couldn't imagine it.

"Emma was four when she said she was happy because she had enough moose wings to help her fly away," said Mo.

"Moose wings?" I said. "What are moose wings?"

Mo slammed on the brakes. Snow and gravel flew. Pulling off her glove, she opened the car door, leaned down, and dug around in the snow. A blast of cold air whipped through the car. I hunched down and breathed warmth onto Belle. I was glad when Mo straightened up and shut the door again.

She grinned and opened her hand to reveal golden brown moosewood seeds. "Moose wings!" she said, like she was sharing a special treasure with me. Mo rolled down the window and, lifting her hand to her mouth, blew lightly. The delicate wings spun in the snowy air and floated down like twirling fairies.

"Fruit of the moosewood tree. Otherwise known as—"

"*Acer pennsylvanicum*. Striped maple," I pronounced with a smile.

"Hey, you're *better* than good at this!" Mo said, rolling the window up and shifting back into first gear. "Emma called this her moose walk. We used to sing to the trees as we walked. And I thought—" Mo stopped abruptly.

I was still amazed that my mom had talked about flying. I waited to hear more.

"Until your mom was fourteen, she said it was her magical path." Mo's voice was quiet.

Until she was fourteen? I thought. *That's only a couple of years older than me! What happened?* But I didn't want to ask. It seemed like an awfully deep subject to get into before we even reached the house.

At the end of the long driveway was an eggplant purple Victorian house with violet trim. We got out of the car, and Mo grabbed my suitcase from the trunk. I held Belle, using my hand to make a little umbrella over her head to protect her from the snow.

I looked up at the crooked house. Each window was a different size and shape, and some of the panes of glass were brilliantly colored. The house had many roofs, all pitched at various angles. Two sugar maples, just like the ones at the beginning of the driveway, grew right through the front porch and porch roof, forming gnarled columns. The porch itself rose and fell above the mounds of their humungous roots.

"Never mind the bumps," Mo said as we went up the uneven steps. "The trees are slowly taking over my porch. And I say, more power to them!" With that, she flung open the double front doors and announced: "Welcome to the Eggplant House."

Once inside, I just stood there, looking around, trying to get my bearings, which was not easy! Every wall was plastered with photographs, postcards, paintings, and handwritten pages. Growing things were everywhere, and not just plants in pots! A beautiful white-flowered vine had pushed its way through a floorboard and wound around the staircase.

"Is that really a *Passiflora*?" I asked Mo.

"Ah, yes, my passion vine," said Mo, dropping the suitcase at the foot of the stairs.

"But it's freezing cold!" I protested, picturing those white flowers sprouting into deep purple passion fruit in a Brazilian jungle, or maybe in Califa, but certainly not in New Jersey, even indoors.

"My dear, it's never winter in the Eggplant House," Mo said. She hung her coat up on a hook shaped like a snake and dropped her gloves on the hissing radiator painted gold. While she pulled off her snowy boots, I set Belle down on a table whose top had sheet music glued to it. I pulled off my gloves and dropped them on the radiator, too. Then I hung my matching spring green jacket on a snake hook beside Mo's and kicked my own boots off to join hers.

Mo smiled at me as she tossed her keys into a basket next to a dusty violin bearing the inscription *Aventurine*. There was something familiar about that word. Was it the name of a long-lost family member my mother mentioned once? Was it a color?

Mo snatched up my suitcase again, carrying it effortlessly up the circular staircase. Her big feet in droopy socks clomped on the steps. I almost giggled at the thought that her plants might tighten up all their roots from the vibration. I picked up Belle and followed, my feet barely making a sound.

I stopped at the crescent-shaped landing halfway up the stairs. It was crammed with old musical instruments webbed with spider's lace. A clarinet rested on the floor next to a broken music stand.

"I know people who would be tempted to give that clarinet a little nudge and watch everything come tumbling down," I said to myself; then I realized I'd actually said it aloud!

"I suppose those are people I would never invite into my home," said Mo.

I reminded myself to stay quiet until the jury was in on whether or not my grandmother was a certifiable C.O.B.

"Do you play?" I asked.

"These old things? No. I need to fix them," she said, nodding toward the instruments. "I have a working violin and guitar," she added.

We climbed the rest of the stairs and Mo turned around, announcing, "This room was your mother's. You may move things around if you want. I left it as it's always been, figuring she'd be back to change it herself someday." Mo swung open the door and stepped back.

Neon pink bedroom walls were plastered with posters of old pop bands. Above the headboard, on the sloping ceiling, were two posters of a teenage boy with shoulder-length blond hair parted down the middle. I checked out the signature at the bottom of the poster.

"Who's Leif Garrett?" I asked.

Mo sighed and playfully rolled her eyes. "He was a singer who was popular for a while. Oh, your mother had such a crush on him." She smiled ruefully. "Closest thing to a plant I could get her to as a teenager was this Leif."

I found myself truly grinning (braces and all) for the first time in weeks. It was just the kind of joke *I* would make! "So she *did* have fun when she was a kid," I said.

Mo looked around the room as if she were hunting for an answer. Then she said, "Probably more than she remembers, Birdie. She's forgotten so much, left it all behind."

My good mood vanished, and suddenly and terribly, I missed Califa and my friends. I missed my dad. I even missed my mom. I put Belle on the nightstand, willing the tears to go away before they spilled over.

"Tomorrow, let's transplant Belle into new . . . uh . . . clothes," Mo suggested. "But I must say, I'm very fond of the hat she's wearing now."

I could tell Mo knew I was sad. But I was still feeling cautious, and I sure didn't want to start crying, so I said, as lightly as possible, "Thanks."

I picked up my suitcase and tossed it on the bed.

"I'll leave you to it," said Mo. And with that, she headed out the door. I could hear her big feet *thump-thump*ing all the way down the stairs.

I sat for a minute, gathering my thoughts. I liked my grandmother. I had to repeat this to myself to make sure I wasn't just imagining things. I *liked* my grandmother. Yes, I liked *my* grandmother, my very own Granny Mo. I liked her a lot. I even liked thinking about calling her the name she wanted me to, Granny Mo, though I'd always think of her as just Mo to myself.

All at once, I knew that I'd much rather be downstairs with her than unpacking my things in this way-too-pink bedroom.

2

The Garden

I went to find Granny Mo, which was easy, since all I had to do was follow the noise. A teapot was sending a piercing whistle up the stairs, pots were clanking, and Mo was singing "Deck the Halls" (even though it was nearly a week after Christmas!). I edged my way down the staircase, through a hall, and into the kitchen, where the racket was coming from.

"Some tea?" Mo asked, even though her back was to me. She turned off the burner of the old-fashioned stove and picked up the screaming red teakettle.

"I guess. I don't know," I said. How had she known I was there? "Do you have hot chocolate?"

"Hot chocolate it is!" She riffled through the cabinets. "But I make awfully good tea, with fruit and flowers in it."

"Tea is fine," I said quickly, since I could see my request was causing quite a ruckus.

"And you need something to put in your stomach. How about grilled cheese?" she asked, slamming a heavy iron skillet down on a burner.

"Great," I said. "Thanks, Granny Mo." Hoping she wouldn't make a big deal out of my deciding what to call her, I crossed to a wide kitchen window made of eyeglass lenses. I looked through them at the snowy landscape beyond. I squeezed one eye shut and peeped through a large monocle at square plots covered in snow. I recognized them as raised flower beds, but there were so many of them that I figured the lens was creating multiple images.

"There's a greenhouse back there at the edge of the ridge on your left," said Mo.

I moved to a pair of pink octagon-shaped lenses to try to see it. Suddenly everything in sight was rose colored.

"That's how I make my living, selling plants and teas from the garden and the greenhouse," Mo said proudly. I smelled the grilled cheese burning, so I figured it was a good thing she hadn't chosen cooking as a career. "The work earns me just enough to keep this old place up and running."

I pressed my nose against the thick pink glass. To my amazement, I saw a spectacularly *grand* Victorian greenhouse with steamy windows, and more snow-covered flower beds, hundreds of trees, an apple orchard, a bridge . . . and—it was the most incredibly huge garden I'd ever in my whole life imagined!

"Can we go see the garden?" I asked.

"You betcha," said Mo. "As soon as we've finished our late lunch and called your father."

Mo was true to her word. After we finished our orange-mint-smelling tea (which was interesting) and our grilled cheese sandwiches (which were crispy charred), and called home and talked to Dad (who promised to send me a good-night e-mail), Mo said, "There's mostly snow out there, but at least I can show you the maze. Come on!"

"Maze?" I asked, hurrying to catch up to her.

She was already over by the snake hooks, buttoning up a furry purple coat, boots back on. She had on fake leopard-fur earmuffs, and that now-familiar grin was back on her face. "At dusk, the temperature starts dropping fast, so grab a scarf and hat," she said. "And why don't you wear my green coat?" With that, she marched back through the kitchen.

I heard the kitchen door slamming behind Mo as I scrambled to put on her coat and my boots. The coat went nearly to my feet and the sleeves were too long, but I rolled them up to reveal a tiger-print lining. How perfect! I shoved my gloves in one of the pockets and grabbed a ski hat with a tassel and a striped scarf, which must have been twelve feet long.

"My Christmas roses are in full swing at this time of year," Mo proudly announced as I stepped outside. She pointed to snowy blossoms while I was still wrapping the scarf around and around my neck. "As I am sure you know, Birdie, *Helleborus niger* is the only true white hellebore. Legend says it sprouted from the tears of a girl who cried in the snow in Bethlehem because she had no gift to give the Baby Jesus."

Evergreens peeked out from under the snow, and rose hips dangled from a hedge like orange and red ornaments. We started down a path, and Mo pointed to the far right. "That's my rock garden with succulent plants," she said. "And over to the left are my vegetable beds."

There was a kitchen garden with scraggly blackberries and raspberries still winding along bamboo teepees, contrasting with limey green brussels sprouts hanging from frozen stalks. Everything looked Christmasy in a pleasantly natural way.

"I'll have some early peas in a few months," Mo went on, tucking a few rose hips into her pocket (no doubt to make a nice pot of tea later). "There will be summer squash and Fourth of July cucumbers and lots of flowers, of course."

The greenhouse rose like a castle. It was a playing field's distance behind the house. Its windows were fogged up, and steam rose from vents in the back corners.

"So, what plants do you grow in there for your business?" I asked.

"I experiment with different things. I love to experiment, don't you?" said Mo. "I meant to tell you, I'm wired for the Internet here, so you can e-mail anytime. I sell my specialties online, and locally, too. I've got the finest white tea in this hemisphere; *Camilla sinensis* grows right in my New Jersey backyard." She chuckled. "An unlikely spot, no?"

"Unlikely?" I repeated, pulling my scarf up. More like *impossible,* since tea usually grows in subtropical places like hot, humid Cambodia.

"Then there are my year-round herbals—I've

got some secret recipes for those." She winked and went on, "Lavender, chamomile, and peppermint. Can you name all of them botanically?"

"Let's see," I said, rising to the challenge. "*Lavandula, Anthemis, Mentha.*"

"Well, aren't you *something!*" she exclaimed.

I smiled shyly, but I could feel myself glowing inside.

"Okay, on to the maze!" Granny Mo said.

I followed Mo as she headed down the path, past the spectacular greenhouse. *Darn!* I thought. I'd been hoping to duck inside. It was now bitter cold as the sun sank to the horizon, and icy snow sprayed off the trees and hills with every gust of wind.

"No time for tinkering today," Mo shouted, her words trailing back to me in a frosty cloud.

The path rose up, up, up, and I was trying to watch my footing on the icy patches as I followed along. Suddenly I came to a screeching halt. The land plunged into a twenty-foot-deep ravine. There was a wooden bridge connecting my side to the lower land on the other side. Did I tell you that I don't like heights? I stood there telling myself: *You're not in Califa anymore. You'll have to get used to ice and all kinds of slippery slopes.*

"Come on, Birdie!" Mo called from up ahead.

"Just take it slow. One step at a time."

I reached down and wiped the snow off the soles of my boots. Now I'd have traction. I took a step and grabbed the handrail, which felt very solid. But when I looked down at that ravine, my whole body started shaking.

"Good girl!" Mo shouted, encouraging me. But as she watched, she could see I wasn't moving. She stomped back over the bridge through the snow like it was nothing and put her hand on mine. "This part of the yard where it drops is called the 'ha-ha,'" she said. I shivered, not seeing the humor. "In Ireland they use ha-has to keep the sheep in the pasture and out of the garden." As she talked, I took my gaze off the drop and looked across the bridge. There was a maze of six-foot-tall boxwood shrubs in the center.

"From the house, you can't see the maze at all, but from this spot it's visible in all its majesty. What a happy surprise, dontcha think?" Mo asked. "That's why I call this the Ha-Ha Valley."

It was majestic, all right. The maze stretched a hundred feet across—a perfect circle of boxwoods with a massive oak tree rising from the center.

"Wow!" I said. I looked at the whole expanse of Mo's land. As wonderful as our garden in Califa had been, Mo's garden was what I had always imagined I'd have when I grew up.

"Come on, I'll point out all the special places as we walk," said Mo. She pressed my hand on the railing, as if to secure me, then let go and took my other hand in hers. Thankfully, she walked slowly this time. I set each step like I had big monster feet, sinking into the crusted snow. I looked ahead, not down.

"Over there is my butterfly meadow," Mo said, pointing to a sea of brown sticks in the snow. "Oh, you should see those colors in midsummer! Blossoms and butterflies everywhere!"

I imagined how beautiful it must be. "Can I come back to see it in the summer?" I asked.

"I would love that!" said Mo, squeezing my hand. "You're doing great. We're already halfway across. Now look over there, beyond that meadow."

I took a deep breath. I *was* doing great. Not needing to hold on to Mo's hand anymore, I kept up my solid, heavy-footed pace as I looked to where Mo was pointing.

"That path leads to a waterfall," said Mo. Off in the distance were miles of forests, backed by jagged, glistening cliffs. "You might want to hike up there. All uphill, but worth it."

Not at sunset, and not in this cold, I thought. I

couldn't even see the waterfall from here, so the hike must be a long one.

"And now look by the apple orchard," Mo continued as I tried to twist my head backward and keep my feet walking forward, not an easy trick. "That's an absolutely magical garden." She leaned back toward me as if she was about to share a deep secret. "In spring and summer, it's like a fairyland."

I knocked the snow off the soles of my boots to get more traction, eying the fairy woodland. Other than the orchard, there was nothing there but snow.

I followed in Mo's footprints, one long-striding step at a time. We finally made it across the bridge, where a short path led to the entrance to the boxwood maze, which was frosted with snow. The sheer size of the hedges, as dense as brick walls, was staggering.

"Can we go in?" I asked.

"Be my guest," said Mo, waving me ahead.

I began the walk through the maze. I chose my steps to keep from slipping in the snow, and chose my turns to avoid dead ends. Mo followed, and when I turned back to look at her, her face was beaming. We made the switchback turns and curves through the maze path. It was absolutely silent in there, insulated by the boxwoods and the snow. All I could hear was the crunching of our boots on the ground.

I picked up my pace, since the snow and the trees had turned a golden pink hue and I knew the sun would be setting any minute. Turn, run, turn, run. Mo's footsteps kept up right behind me, and then . . .

There I stood in the center of the maze, feeling very tiny (minuscule, actually) beneath the biggest deciduous tree I'd ever laid eyes on. Back home in Califa, we had some good-sized native oaks, but I'd never ever seen one this huge! The trunk was as massive as a giant sequoia; there was no way my arms could ever reach around it. The bark was rough with furrows and ridges, like a wise old face. Even in this wintry air, the tree felt welcoming and warm.

"How do you do, Ms. Quercus?" I asked the tree, extending a bow.

"*Quercus robur!*" exclaimed Mo with surprise. "Of course, it's an English oak!" She stared up at the tree herself for a few moments. "I've always just called it the Glimmer Tree."

"How come?" I asked.

"My grandmother named it that," Mo replied. "I used to climb it, and so did your mother when she was little."

We stood silently as the tree's powerful limbs rustled in the wind, casting shadows against the pale pink background of the December sky. Suddenly I couldn't help but wrap my arms around the huge trunk, as far as I could reach. The tree somehow made everything seem safe and good and, well, like everything would be okay, even if things felt hard now.

"Your mother loved this tree," said Mo, as if hugging a tree was the most natural thing in the world. "She thought Glimmer was a perfect name, and she always said the sun made its leaves glimmer like stars."

"Seems awfully poetic for the Mom *I* know," I said, running my fingers along one of the tree's many knotholes.

"Well, loving trees is a family thing," said Mo. "Hard to shake, even for someone like your mother. My grandmother, who was your great-great-grandmother Dora, was an arborist, a tree girl with a wild and colorful imagination. You have the gift, too," Mo said with a wink.

I made my way to the tree's other side and hugged again. My face rested on a spot that felt oddly mushy. I reached up and wiped the snow off. There was a large section of bark that was soft compared to the rest, as if it were rotting or sick or something.

"Look at this, Granny Mo!" I exclaimed. "I think the tree might be sick!"

She came to my side and felt the area, nodding slowly, her mouth oddly pinched. "Yes, I've been worried about that," she said sadly. She sighed. "It started years ago, Birdie. It was just a tiny patch, but it has been growing worse year by year. The damage goes deeper than what you see."

"Yes, it probably goes down to the roots, Granny Mo," I said.

"Exactly," she agreed. "The roots. We've inherited the job of taking care of all green life. We sing the green song. And you are the strongest member of the Arbor Lineage now, Birdie. It's up to you."

I got a shiver up and down my spine, and it wasn't from the cold.

"Me?" I asked. "What are you talking about? What do I have to do with the Glimmer Tree rotting?"

"Well, to tell you the honest truth—everything,"

said Mo. "You didn't cause it, but you do have the power to heal it. You have the gift, Birdie, in spades."

I started wondering about Mo's crazy streak and was relieved when a fluffy Siamese cat trotted out from behind the Glimmer Tree. He rubbed against Mo's boot.

"Ah, there you are, Willowby. You're hungry, eh?" said Mo. "He loves to hide in the ferns out here in the summer . . . a whole world of ferns around the base of this tree." She picked him up and growled in his face, then looked at me. "But summer or winter, he's a cranky old cat when he wants to eat. You'll have to forgive his rude behavior for now. Come on, let's head home."

Mo led the way back, me and Wil-lowby right on her heels. Mo was silent on the way, though she waited patiently for me to cross the bridge again. I decided not to mention the odd things she'd said. She was clearly a unique person, but I wasn't sure I was ready for her to be quite so . . . weird.

My fingers, toes, and nose felt like ice

cubes by the time we got back. Granny Mo and I settled into two comfy chairs in her living room (no TV in sight) and had dinner right in front of the fire, warming our feet while we ate. After all that walking in the cold, Mo's tomato soup with fresh basil and burnt croutons was the most delicious meal I had ever had. Antiques crammed the fireplace mantel and window ledges in the living room. There were porcelain doodads set on every surface, and every kind of clock you can imagine was *tick-tock*ing up and down the walls.

Once Willowby had decided I was trustworthy (his attitude no doubt related to his full belly), he curled up in my lap, purring. We were all ready for an early bedtime.

"Now don't stay up reading too late, and turn off the lights before you go upstairs," Mo warned as she gave me and Willowby a couple of pecks on the tops of our heads, picked up our dishes, and headed back to the kitchen. "Sweet dreams, Birdie dear!" she called as I heard her go up the stairs.

No worries about reading, since I could barely keep my eyes open. I took five minutes to just enjoy being alone, then I moved Willowby to the couch, turned off several lamps, and headed upstairs myself.

In my mother's old room, I threw my suitcase

on a chair, opened it, and changed into cozy thermals. I flopped down on the bed. I propped my laptop on a pillow, flicked it on, and checked my e-mail. There was a message from my dad that complimented me on how cool I was, going off to meet Granny Mo on my own, and updated me on Mom's news from London, and ended with "Love you, my Redbird. Dad. P.S. Mom's okay with what you're doing, too. She wasn't very happy at first, but she recognizes that this is part of your growing up and you need to know your family, especially with the move."

"I love you, too, my one and only dad," I replied in an e-mail. I added some stuff about the train ride and Granny Mo, but I didn't tell him about the Glimmer Tree. Somehow it seemed too secret to be sending off into cyberspace. I glanced up from the computer. Something was distracting me. Ah, the posters. I stood on the mattress, pulled down Leif and his fake smile, rolled him up, and pushed him under the bed. He wasn't *my* dream.

When I stood up, a fierce blast of cold air shot into the room. The old window overlooking Mo's garden rattled. I grabbed a blanket off the foot of the bed to stick into the cracks on both sides of the window. I looked outside; the beauty of the night sky took my breath away. I imagined my mother as a girl, standing in this same place, looking out at the tip-top of the Glimmer Tree, way off in the strange and beautiful Ha-Ha Valley. Was that tree the last place Mom allowed herself to get lost in imagination?

The wind swept the clouds away. I watched the constellations appear, like Dad and I used to do on camping trips. There was Orion and there was Andromeda, and then . . . the stars began to move. Really! The stars from Orion's belt zipped along in a trio, Andromeda played with the Northern Crown, and hundreds, maybe thousands of stars danced right there in the yard. I shut my eyes tight, and when I opened them, I looked back up to the sky. Every constellation and every star except for one sparkled back in their proper places.

A sense of foreboding creeped across my skin. I stuffed the edges of the blanket into the window frame, and then turned back to the bed.

At the end of the bed, where I had just taken away the blanket, was a book—a *huge* book, the size of a really big dictionary. It was clearly handmade, and so yellowed and tattered it could be a thousand years old. How could I not have seen it?

I spun around, expecting Granny Mo to be in the room, even though I'd shut the door. How did she get this book into my room? There was no doubt in my mind that she'd put it there. "Don't stay up too late reading," she'd warned.

I picked up the book, which weighed more than Willowby, and snuggled down under the comforter. I stared at the ornate cover: *The Book of Dreams.* The size of the book made it clear that the author had sure dreamed a lot. I ran my fingers along the silver, shimmering script, and then along the thick binding. I took a deep breath, opened the cover, and began leafing through the pages.

Violets, roses, and four-leaf clovers were pressed onto yellowed pages. There were poetic entries, musical notations, recipes, crocheted bookmarks with girls' names on them, and what looked like mathematical equations. Some pages were stuck together as if the years had sealed them tight, and still others were indecipherable, as if rain had run the words together.

I took my hands off the book. I didn't know where to begin. That's when I made my decision to let the book show me the way. I shut the book, closed my eyes, and opened the book to a random page.

July 15, 1929

I am lying under the stars like I always do, except I am still in my nightgown. I am not cold at all. The stars are millions of tiny dots in the sky. All of a sudden, they move closer, and it looks like they are coming right for me. I look down and realize that I am flying!!

Afraid I might fall, I carefully twirl around until I see the whole garden and my house below, dark and fast asleep. Then one of the stars buzzes in front of my face, and I see it is a tiny firefly. It perches on my nose, and I know that it is special. Then it flies in front of me, as if to let me know it is safe to fly into this mysterious glimmering space.

I give up my fear. We fly together, the firefly and me. The sky around us changes from dark blue, to purple, to deep green. We fly so fast we must look like shooting stars.

Dora

3

The Singing Stone

Gong! Buzz! Cuckoo!

I bolted upright in the dark. It sounded like all the clocks in the living room were going off at once! I jumped out of bed, remembering the book when my feet touched the cold floor. I turned back to see if the book was still there or if I had dreamed it. There it was, right on my pillow. Wow.

I pulled a pair of socks from my suitcase, put them on, and tiptoed down the stairs in the dark. The second I walked into the living room, the clocks fell silent.

I squinted to read the time on an old carved clock on the mantel. Three a.m.! I shivered and was just turning to go back upstairs when another clock caught my eye. It read 12:00. It wasn't noon, and it couldn't be midnight, because the sun's rays were just peeking in the window. I looked around. The cuckoo clock said 1:05. The grandfather clock, its brass pendulum still swinging, said 9:27.

Lilium tigrinum obviously didn't give a hoot about keeping time. Just then, Granny Mo shuffled out from the kitchen, wearing a flowered apron over her sweater and jeans.

"Didn't you hear the clocks?" I asked.

"Oh! Those crazy old things; I always ignore them," Mo said, dismissing the problem with a wave of her spatula. "But I should have warned you. They all chime at seven a.m., sharp. Never fail! No matter what time they say. Oh yes, and at two in the afternoon on Leap Day—February twenty-ninth, every fourth year. Never knew why. Still don't. Well, anyway, come to the kitchen. I'm making breakfast." With that, she sailed back to the kitchen and turned up the music.

I followed in time to catch her singing: *"Oh, you better not pout, I'm telling you why, Santa Claus is comin'..."*

Mo sang along with the radio (and why were they playing Christmas songs after Christmas?), her voice cracking on the high notes. Willowby, sitting on the kitchen table, joined in with an occasional *meow.*

"I hope you like blueberry pancakes," Mo said while she ladled big disks of batter onto a skillet, leaving a trail of drips on the stove.

"I sure do," I said.

"And elderberry tea," she added. I didn't answer. Mo chuckled. "I'll get you to be a real tea drinker sooner or later. But you're young still. In the meantime, pour yourself some orange juice. Fresh picked and squeezed this morning!" I got a glass of juice but didn't ask how she could have picked the oranges this morning.

Mo started setting the kitchen table, singing about being good, for goodness' sake. I liked it. We didn't sing much around our house, and it felt kind of good to hear her just belting it out. I noticed smoke pouring from the iron skillet, so I grabbed the spatula, flipped the pancakes, and turned off the burner. Singing right along with Mo and the radio now, I tossed the hot pancakes onto our plates.

"So, tell me something about *The Book of Dreams*," I said as I sat down and poured syrup on my pancakes. I thought Granny Mo was going to choke on her blueberries when I said it. "You put that book in my room, didn't you?" I asked.

"It's not from me," she said. A big grin was growing on her face. "But it has the most beautiful writing on the cover, doesn't it?"

"But if *you* didn't put it there," I said, "then how . . . who?"

"It must be the fairies," Mo said. Her eyes were sparkling in a way that I hadn't seen before.

"Excuse me?" I said. "Fairies?"

Mo leaned over. Her green eyes were so close to mine that I started going cross-eyed. I sat back in my chair a bit. "The fairies are the keepers of the book. Don't you see?" she asked.

I shook my head. I didn't see, but I could feel myself starting to get excited anyway. I couldn't help it—what would you do if someone told you fairies were real, and clearly believed it themselves?

"Fairies?" I asked again, trying hard to sound normal.

"Oh, there's so much ahead of you," Mo said. "The last time—" Suddenly her eyes filled with tears, but she blinked them away. "Where is the book?"

"In my room," I said. I was feeling a little tense, like, what do I do now? I decided that I'd just follow Mo's lead. I was clearly in over my head on this one.

"Well, what are we waiting for?" Mo asked, cramming the last of her pancakes into her mouth like a little kid.

Taking the stairs two at a time, I raced upstairs

with Mo right behind me. I admit it: I had given in to the excitement and the idea of fairies being real! I threw open the bedroom door. The room was filled with the scent of lilacs.

"Fairy magic almost always brings that smell!" whispered Mo, sniffing the air.

I glanced around the room but saw no flowers or fairies. There was something else I didn't see either.

"It's gone!" I said. It wasn't where I'd left it. I checked under the pillow and then threw back the covers. It was absolutely, positively gone! I looked over at Mo; her expression had turned thoughtful, but I wanted to know what had happened!

Rustle, rustle, I heard. I went toward the window where the sound was coming from. I ripped down the blanket I'd stuffed into the cracks last night and threw it on the bed. There, fluttering in the cold breeze, stuck between the window and the sill, was a cream-colored envelope. I pulled it out. I recognized it; it had been tucked inside the front cover of *The Book of Dreams.*

I looked from the gray sky out toward the Glimmer Tree. I held up the envelope.

"Oh, yes . . . the tree," Mo whispered.

"The . . . tree?" I asked. Carefully, I ran my

fingernail along the silver wax seal. When it loosened, I held my breath and opened the flap.

"Yes, we have many things to talk about, Birdie dear. But I've got a couple of guys coming to deliver fertilizer and potting soil in a few minutes," she said. "Believe it or not, the fairies can wait while we take care of some present responsibilities. Come out to the greenhouse with me?"

"Ummm, yeah. Sure," I said. I didn't want to wait at all, but I didn't know Mo well enough to argue with her—not yet.

"Bring the letter," said Mo.

Totally curious, I put on my jeans right over my thermals and put the envelope into my back pocket. Mo had been so serious, I was a little afraid of it now. Maybe the whole thing was a joke or something cute Mo had thought I'd like because I was a kid. Or what if my mother was right, and Mo was certifiable? In that case, I guess the worst I'd have to do was play along with the fairies game. Or was it a game? I really didn't know.

I caught up with Mo by the snake hooks. I pulled on my boots, then grabbed the long scarf, a ski hat, and my gloves. I threw on Mo's big green coat again and managed to follow in her footsteps as she clomped through the kitchen. Willowby joined us as we walked out and along the path.

The steamy double doors of the greenhouse opened into a heaven of green and glass and stillness. A table of succulents sat inside the doorway next to another coatrack, this one with butterfly hooks. I followed Mo and hung up my coat and scarf, then replaced my winter gloves with the gardening gloves that she handed me.

Unseen droplets of water echoed as I gazed at aisles of plants that reached to the right and left. Orchids and bromeliads hung from ceiling wires. There were long tables of hothouse tomatoes and special areas for baby tea plants. Ten full-sized orange trees stood together. Behind the orange trees was a small room.

"What's that room for?" I asked, pointing.

"That's where I live a lot of the spring and summer," said Mo. "There's a little kitchen, a cot, my favorite reading chair, and all my favorite books. Go take a look."

As she cut a few white lilies and arranged them in a vase, I wandered into the alcove, rolling up my sleeves in the warmth. The books were all about organic farming and composting, herbs and teas and exotic spices (nothing about fairies). On a table beside the chair upholstered with a giant-leaf-patterned fabric sat a real bird's nest with an egg inside.

I gently lifted the egg out and saw it was not an egg at all, but a smooth, grayish-blue stone that fit perfectly in the palm of my hand. Half of it was missing, leaving a jagged edge along the side. I turned the stone over in my hand and found a drawing in black on the other side. Even though it was only half an image, it was clear it was a maze.

I brushed the carving with one finger. A tingle spread through my body. I hummed the little melody that came to my mind. Beyond the rhythm I could feel a whole tune coming from inside me.

From her lily-arranging table, Mo started to hum along with me. It was as if we had both known this song our whole lives. Suddenly the tune petered out in my head. It must have petered out in Mo's head, too, because she stopped humming at the same time.

"That song comes from the Singing Stone," said Mo.

"This?" I asked, holding up the broken stone.

Mo glanced over and nodded. "Exactly."

I waited quietly to hear more. This trip was turning out

to be anything but your typical weekend over-the-river-and-through-the-woods-to-Grandmother's-house-we-go.

"Used to be a seed, actually, that stone," Mo said, her eyes on the lilies in the vase. "It was a special acorn that fell from a tree in a place called Aventurine."

I turned it over in my hand. *A petrified seed*, I thought. "The name of your old violin?" I asked.

Mo seemed pleased that I had noticed. "Yes," she said with a little smile. She stood back to admire her lilies. "You can see that the stone is broken in half," Mo went on. "I've been getting the feeling that soon it will be whole again."

"Do *I* have something to do with that feeling you're getting?" I asked, staring at the half-stone and feeling light-headed and slightly queasy. Was I ready for the answer? I had read *Harry Potter* along with all my friends, but that was a book. This was my life!

Suddenly Mo was at the doorway of the little room. "Yes, my Birdie, my very special grand-daughter, you do," she answered.

My gaze shot up to meet hers, and I stood straighter when I saw the pride there.

"You *know* you've come here for a reason, don't you?" she asked. "And it wasn't just to meet me." Mo motioned to me, and I followed her, the stone cradled in my hand. She led me to a long work counter that was covered with odd mechanical devices and what looked like dried tea leaves.

"I don't suppose you have a tea potion that might fix the rot on that tree?" I said.

Mo let out a little chuckle. "Oh, if it were only that easy!" she said.

"So why *am* I here, Granny Mo?" I asked, looking at the stone again.

"To heal that wound you found yesterday in the Glimmer Tree. The rotting," she said. She started sweeping dried tea leaves into neat little mounds with a piece of white paper. "And to find the other half of the Singing Stone, and to help put our family back together."

"And how am I supposed to do that?" I whispered. Suddenly I felt more worried than I ever had in my whole life. This whole business of fairies, Mom, Mo, the book, and the stone was all a jumble. Something important was happening to me, I could feel it.

I leaned against a small tree beside the long table, then looked up as its bark caught at my shirt. Its bark was scarlet and peeling, and its brilliant green leaves were shaped like clubs and hearts on playing cards. "Gumbo-limbo," I said automatically. *"Bursera simaruba."*

Mo nodded. "A miracle healer when made into tea," she said, picking up a handful of the leaves and tossing them into one of her contraptions. "By the way," she added, packing the gumbo-limbo leaves down with her thumb, "that letter the fairies left will probably help explain some of this."

"Oh, the envelope!" I exclaimed. I put down the Singing Stone (how easily I had accepted the name!) and dug in my pocket. But just as I pulled out the envelope, a flatbed truck pulled up, its brakes making an earsplitting screech.

"Hold that thought," said Mo, giving my shoulder a squeeze as she dashed to the door. "It's my delivery guys."

She waved to two burly men dressed in thick woolen hats and jackets, their complexions rosy. They lumbered inside to greet her with hearty hugs. I pushed the envelope back into my pocket.

"Travis, I want you to meet my granddaughter, Birdie," Mo announced proudly.

The guy named Travis shook hands with me. "Hey, Birdie, so glad to meet you," he said. His big hand swallowed mine as cold air poured off his woolly clothes. "Your grandmother is one of our favorite people in all of Colts Ridge. This here's Hank."

"Kind of a chip off the old block, ain't she?" said Hank, speaking to Mo. "She's got your eyes and hair." Then he turned to me and vigorously shook my hand as well. "You got her green thumb, too?"

"I guess so," I said. I tried to act friendly, but I didn't know what to say, and I certainly wasn't going to smile enough for my braces to show.

"Hank and Travis will be helping me for a few hours, so it's fine to wander off and explore," said Mo.

"I promised your grandma we'd help out if she'd let me take her out tonight for New Year's Eve," Hank announced, grinning at me. I actually saw a blush come over my grandmother's face.

The guys started hauling bags of soil over their shoulders and heaving them onto the floor of the entryway.

Mo pulled me aside before she went to join them. "You might want to take a stroll up to the waterfall," she whispered.

Cold air was blasting in through the door, so Mo went over and pulled a big sheet of plastic down at the end of the entry. "Meet me at the house for a cup of tea around four o'clock, Birdie," she called, counting the bags. "How's that sound?"

"Okay," I said, feeling anything but okay. "See you at four." What could I do? I bundled back up, wrapping the long, long scarf around my neck. I slipped the stone into one of the pockets of my jeans and headed out into the frosty air, Willowby on my heels.

"See ya soon, Birdie!" called Hank.

"And, Birdie?" called Mo.

I turned around in the open doorway.

"Open that letter while you're in the gardens. I think you were meant to," said Mo. "Good luck!"

"And stay out of trouble, now, you hear?" Travis joked. "Your grandmother causes plenty of trouble for all of us already!"

I believe you're right about that, I thought. I crunched along the gravel path, forgetting both the stone and the envelope for a while as I took in the gardens.

There was the weedy butterfly garden and then the edge of the ravine, where I had the same tingly feeling in my hands and feet as I viewed the Ha-Ha Valley, the maze, and the Glimmer Tree. There, the path forked. I could cross the bridge down to the valley or I could head toward the waterfall Granny Mo had pointed out yesterday.

Willowby circled my boots once and then

headed over the bridge, glancing back at me as if to see where I was headed. The sun was high in the sky, so I knew I had lots of time. I decided to look for the waterfall as Mo had suggested.

I passed a pond, which was frozen solid, and saw the apple orchard by the distant back fence. A trail meandered up into the rocky hills and cliffs, far to the edge of the property. Hiking up the trail, I breathed in the sharp, clean air. Maple trees with their bare branches stood tall against the blue sky, and a patch of willows hung their long, thin branches sadly. Soon I entered an evergreen grove.

I twisted and turned along the path, breathing in its Christmas pine scent, until it broke open to an area covered with enormous boulders, all glazed with a layer of ice. Behind them, as tall as a two-story house, the waterfall came into view. I couldn't hear any splashing water, probably because it was still quite far away. If I wanted to continue on the path, I'd have to climb the boulders.

I sighed. Now that I'd be living through northeast winters, I figured I'd have to learn how to walk on snow and ice. I loved being outdoors, and I wasn't exactly planning to spend November through March inside our city apartment.

"Boulder number one," I said out loud, staring at my first challenge. I placed one foot on the rock, and it immediately slid off like butter on a hot bun. Standing back on both feet, I considered another method. I decided the best way was to carefully wedge my boots into the crevices between the boulders and avoid the flat icy surfaces. I stuck my left foot between two boulders. Once it felt solid, I leaned against the rock, lifted my right foot to another crevice, and wedged it in hard. I lifted my left foot to a higher spot. Nice! It was working. I was moving up. I realized I'd started whistling a little tune. Wedge, lift, and move up. Wedge, lift . . .

I scaled the rocks, one careful foothold at a time, using my hands for stability. Every once in a while, the fingers of my gloves stuck in the sun-glazed ice, and I breathed on them to melt them free. I caught my boot in a tight crevice once or twice and twisted my foot, but nothing too terrible. I was feeling like an adventurer. As I got closer, I realized why there was no splashing sound from the waterfall: It was frozen solid. Ice hung like great long fangs.

I kept climbing until I came to a hollowed rock alcove, right at the base of the falls. To my surprise, two flat boulders there had been fashioned into a stone seat, backrest and all. I sat down, tuckered out and actually sweaty from the climb. Since I'd never touched a frozen waterfall, I took off my gloves, reached up, and ran my hands along the toothy icicles, as slippery-smooth as glass.

If it weren't for the evergreens, my view from there would have been awesome: the whole expanse of Mo's garden. But I was satisfied with the spot I'd discovered: secret bench, snowy trees, and frozen waterfall.

I reached inside the pocket of Mo's coat and pulled out the envelope from *The Book of Dreams*. I waited a moment, holding my breath. Finally I opened it and delicately unfolded the fragile page inside. It was a drawing of a tree with names on its branches: a family tree. Under the tree were the words *The Arbor Lineage*.

My eyes shot directly to my own name: Birdie Cramer Bright. How did *my* name get on this old family tree? Or was this drawing some kind of fairy magic that would lead me to . . . I wished I knew more!

On one branch I found Dora, my great-great-grandmother born in 1916. Jean Cramer was next, but her name was stricken through in red ink. She must have been Mo's mother, and I remember hearing that she died when Mo was very young. More names followed, all with birth years beside them. There was Maureen, who was Granny Mo, of course, b. 1939. Emma P. Cramer was listed next. My breath caught in my throat when I saw that my mother's name had been crossed out, just like Jean's, but in silvery pencil. What did that mean?

I folded the paper back into the envelope and tucked it safely in my coat pocket. Then I closed my eyes. Leaning back on the stone seat, I put my hands in my pockets. My left hand grasped the broken Singing Stone.

The stone's rhythm and tune rose and vibrated into my heart.

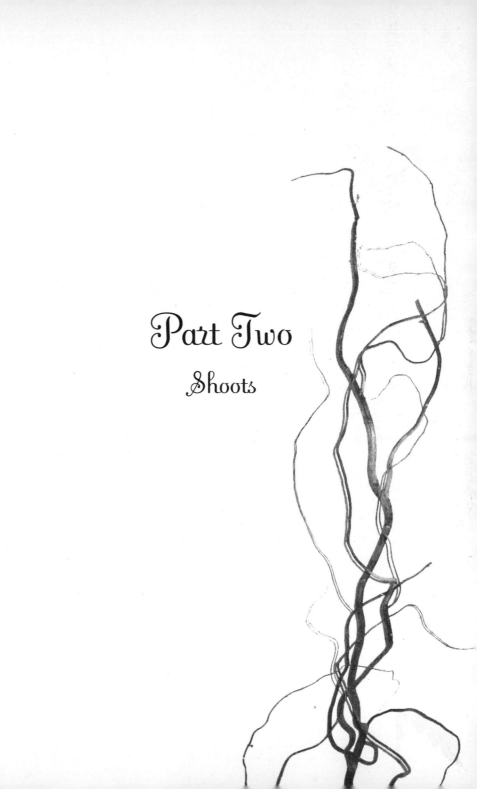

Part Two
Shoots

4

Aventurine

I opened my eyes as a wild wind swept away the clouds and the sun-filled sky turned bright, bright blue. Suddenly the snow on the evergreens and the ice on the boulders began to melt so fast that water trickled beneath my feet and down toward the trees below. I sank back onto the stone bench in surprise. A light breeze grazed my face and hair and hands, carrying not even a hint of a chill.

It was as if spring was spontaneously shooting into fast-forward all around me. The frozen willows and maples below began to explode with buds, which sprang into fresh leaves, which were electric green. Trees and bushes burst into life so fast, I could hear them growing, inch by inch.

Tiny flowers sprouted up between the cracks in the boulders, and the sweet smell of roses and lilies of the valley wafted through the air. Life gushed and leapt all around me. The Singing Stone's tune was in the wind, the trees, the flowers, and the water rushing behind me.

Water was rushing behind me? I spun around on the rock seat, which was still there, thankfully, solid underneath me. The waterfall had melted and was cascading in sheets of turquoise water down from the rocky hill.

In between, birds warbled, bees and dragonflies buzzed. Then I heard a splash. It was different from the crashing of the waterfall, a *plop*, as if a fish had jumped nearby. Next I heard a giggle, then a mournful noise like bells and whale calls mixed into one sound.

I followed the sound. Just around a tumble of red rocks was a blue pool with layered falls, each dropping gracefully into sunlit rippling waves. Beneath the waves were long, flowing wisps of red, violet, and green. I thought the wisps were algae until the colorful strands came out of the water, and I saw that it was the hair of three beautiful women. Well, they weren't exactly women, since instead of legs they had tails that shimmered in the sunlight. They gazed at me, and I gasped with wonder—mermaids!

Each wore crowns of flowers, gems, and shells

in her hair, and their skin ranged from pale white to riverbank brown. The brownest swam closer to the shore. Her purple hair was as long as her body.

I shook my head, trying to wake up. My eyes must have looked like a little kid's eyes on Christmas morning, full of awe and amazement. I *had* to be dreaming, even though it was beyond me how I could have fallen asleep in the cold. Yet I knew for sure I was dreaming when I saw I was no longer bundled up in my scarf and Mo's coat. I was wearing the same jeans, but I had on my favorite soft T-shirt. I would have frozen to death in Mo's winter garden in that outfit!

The woman—or rather, the mermaid—nearest to me blinked her chocolate brown eyes. They changed to violet, matching her mass of hair. She held out her hand, as if I was supposed to touch it or kiss it. I reached out to shake hands. Her skin was cool and wet. When I touched her, I was amazed to watch her hair lighten to glowing green. She let out a kind of watery sigh, then spoke in some trilling, musical language.

I *wanted* to understand her. It sounded like she was saying something important. It was as if I'd stepped into a fairy-tale book with beautiful water-color illustrations, and I desperately wanted to be a part of it.

"Excuse me?" I said. "I don't understand." I was hoping that since I was dreaming, the words would come out in her trilling music, but they were in English, in my own voice.

The other two mermaids swam closer. One had waist-length red hair, green eyes, and skin the color of moonlight. She had a three-part tail that must have made her a fast swimmer. The other had full lips and aquamarine eyes framed with lashes that quivered with sparkling drops of water like diamonds. The violet mermaid batted her eyes several times at me, giggling all the while, and then fanned out her hair in a wide arc in the water, turning it a bright tangerine color. It appeared to be a gesture of welcome.

"Where I come from we have legends about them," came a voice from behind me.

I spun around but saw no one.

The voice spoke again: "They coax children to ride on their backs and then they dive down deep and drown them." It was a girl's strong voice.

I took a few steps toward the red rocks and looked around the flowering plants. There was a girl a little taller than me, practicing a dance of some kind with a foot-long orange-colored stick. She stared into my eyes as she waved and whooshed the stick through the air, making it whistle like a swift wind.

I instantly thought: *Leontopodium alpinum,* a lion's foot, or edelweiss, which is a white flower that grows through the snow, high on mountains like the Alps — beautiful and as strong as steel.

The girl was wearing jeans and a loose T-shirt. Her blond hair was braided and coiled around her head. She stopped swinging the stick and strode toward me. Then she smiled and put out her hand. "Hello, I'm Kerka," she announced with a smile that made me like her.

I shook her hand. She had a firm grip! "I'm Birdie," I said.

"I think I am here to help you in Aventurine," she said.

"What? Where?" I asked.

"Here. Where you are right now. Aventurine."

Suddenly it clicked. Aventurine was the name on Mo's violin, the place where Dora found the acorn that became the Singing Stone. The Singing Stone! I dug into my pocket and was relieved to feel the half-stone. Then I felt around in all my pockets for the envelope, but it was gone.

"I'm in . . . we're in . . . a dream, right?" I asked. "Or a dream world."

"A land for only the strongest dreamers," said Kerka. "Dreamers with destinies."

I turned to look at the mermaids, who were as dreamy as it gets. "Do you know what they were saying?" I asked Kerka.

"No. They don't speak Fairen—the fairy language—as you and I do in Aventurine. My mother told me that even the fairies have to study the language of the river maidens to learn it. That's what they're called, you know, not mermaids. Mermaids only live in salt water, and river maidens live in, well, *rivers*," she explained, digging the tip of her dancing stick into the mossy ground at her feet.

"Ah, river maidens," I repeated, thinking that at least the magic dreaming took care of the language barrier that might be between Kerka and me in the real world.

"And don't let them hear you call them mermaids," she whispered to me. "They'll be terribly insulted. At least that's what my mother said."

I nodded. "And I don't suppose we should be insulting magical creatures," I said. "Even in a dream."

"You got that right," said Kerka. Her eyes were as blue as the sky. She put her hand on the side of her mouth and whispered to me, "They're rather vain, in case you didn't notice."

I'd noticed. Now the three river maidens were

preening and gazing at their reflections in the water. They all talked, as if sharing private jokes.

"So how can I help you?" Kerka asked me.

"I . . . well." I glanced around at the shimmering maiden tails and the rushing waterfall, the blue sky and swaying evergreens. Everything looked so peaceful, it was hard to imagine that I was here on some quest and might need help. "I don't really know," I said. "Do you?"

Kerka leaned her chin on her orange stick, stumped. "My mother told my sisters and me a little about Aventurine, but this is my first time here," she said. "My mother is dead now."

"Oh, I'm really sorry," I said, a little startled at the blunt way she said it.

But that clearly wasn't her point, because she continued immediately. "A few nights ago, I fell asleep with my Kalis stick under my pillow," she said, patting the orange stick. "I came here—to Aventurine, but somewhere different in Aventurine. A voice told me that I had to keep sleeping with my Kalis stick under my pillow, and that I would come here again to help a girl named Birdie heal a stone."

"Yes!" I said in surprise. I pulled the stone from my pocket. "I'm Birdie and this is the Singing Stone!

But it's broken, missing a half. Do you know what I should do?"

Kerka shook her head. "No, but the voice said that I had to help you, so can you tell me a little more about the Singing Stone?"

I sat down at the edge of the pond. Kerka sat beside me. "Well, on the Singing Stone is a picture of a maze with a tree." I held up the half and showed Kerka the picture. She nodded and I went on. "And my granny Mo's garden also has a maze with an incredibly huge tree. Mo calls it the Glimmer Tree. There's a big soft spot on the Glimmer Tree—part of the trunk is rotting and it's getting worse. And then there's my family tree with two names crossed off. Mo said something about fixing the Singing Stone, finding the other half." I remembered one more thing: "And the fairies left a book for me!"

"Then my guess is that the fairies know what you need to do," said Kerka. She stood and started pacing. "My mother told us that Aventurine is filled with fairies, so we just have to go find some!"

The river maidens started splashing a lot, so Kerka and I looked over at them. They were leaping in and out of the water like dolphins, hair flying and all five tails shimmering.

"Okay," I said. "So *how* do we find the fairies?"

"I don't know everything," said Kerka quietly. She suddenly brightened and held up a finger. "The voice said something about looking in my backpack when I met you." (*How could she have forgotten that?*, I wondered, but decided that I really didn't know her well enough to ask her.)

Kerka set her backpack on the ground and rummaged through it. Eventually she pulled out a large rolled-up piece of paper, tied with a red string. She untied the string and then unrolled the paper.

We knelt and spread it out on the ground, each holding an edge as we examined the paper. The paper itself was parchmenty, that kind of yellowed color that old paper gets. On it was a colored-pencil drawing of a girl sitting at a table. The girl was about the same age as Kerka and me, with dark golden skin and curly black hair. It appeared that she was looking at a map. No, she was *making* the map!

"How's that supposed to help?" said Kerka.

The maidens hummed a little tune. We looked over at them again. They were slumped on the pool's edge, their heads cupped in their hands in what looked like disappointment.

Just as I was about to say something, the drawing faded.

"What do we do now?" I wondered, trying not to be too discouraged.

"Wait, look," Kerka said. And we watched as another drawing slowly surfaced, just as if it were coming up from a pool of brown water.

The words "Zally's Map" began to appear, letter by letter, across the top of the paper. I shook my head. This magic stuff was mind-boggling!

"Do you think that girl was Zally?" I asked.

"Maybe," said Kerka. "Probably. But more importantly, this is definitely a map, and maps are always helpful." She leaned in closer, then pulled back quickly as a silent shower of red-gold sparks suddenly flew from the center of the map.

"Yikes!" yelled Kerka as I jumped back, too.

The sparks gathered together over the map and formed words:

Sister dreamers,

This is the only map of Aventurine. I hope it helps you on your quest. Aventurine's geography can change for each dream or dreamer, so this map is not the kind of map you are used to.

Zally

As soon as we had read it, the spark words disbanded and fell back into the map as silently as they had come. Kerka and I carefully leaned back in to look at the map. It was clearer now.

"Look!" Kerka pointed out a tiny drawing of three river maidens in a pool beside the waterfall. "That's where we are now."

Silent sparks flew up from the map once more, and we leapt backward again. This time the sparks were different hues of pink. Instead of making words, they gathered over the map to form a magnificent pink flower, almost as clear as a photograph.

"It's an Agminium," I told Kerka. "It's an extinct species that lived in Califa . . . uh . . . California a thousand years ago."

The pink sparks exploded over the map like a small silent firework and disappeared.

Kerka frowned. "Very nice and pretty, but what does it mean? How will it get us to the fairies?"

Suddenly I was aware of a lot of splashing. The three maidens were clearly still trying to get our attention. They kept diving underwater, and each time they surfaced, all three had changed the colors of their hair (again!). I waved my hand at them, and they gathered at the edge of the pool.

"They're trying to tell us they know something,"

I said to Kerka as I walked over to the river maidens.

Kerka had her nose back in the map. "It looks like we have to swim down into the pond and through a river tunnel to get to that pink flower," she said. "That must be what the map meant by making the flower like that."

By now, the river maidens were reaching for my hands. They wanted me to jump in the water with them! I held back and looked questioningly at Kerka. "What do you think?" I asked.

Kerka shrugged and came over to the water holding the map. Then she bent to show it to the river maidens, pointing to an image of the Agminium flower that had just appeared on the map. The maidens nodded, shaking the shells on their crowns.

"Shall we follow them?" asked Kerka.

"What about those stories of river maidens who coax children into the water and then drown them?" I reminded her.

Kerka grinned sheepishly. "Just Finnish legends meant to scare little kids and keep them out of the water. Sorry," she said.

"That's okay," I said. "I kinda wondered about that." I laughed, watching as Kerka rolled up the map, tied it, and stowed it back in her pack. I was beginning to like her for real.

I went to roll up my jeans to prepare to lower myself gently into the pond, but before I could do it, the three maidens reached out and touched my arms. Suddenly I found myself in the water. I kicked out, expecting to feel my boots heavy on my feet. Instead, I moved easily.

I looked down to find that my clothes had turned into something like a bright green wet suit (although it was a material I'd never seen before), complete with flippers. "Come on, Kerka!" I called, splashing. "The water's great! It's warm and kind of bubbly! And your clothes will change into a wet suit!"

"I can't," Kerka replied. She was standing on the edge of the bank now, wiping her hands on her jeans and biting her lip.

I swam up to the bank. "What do you mean?" Was she deserting me? Already?

"I can't swim," she said. She looked miserable.

"I'm sure you can learn," I said. "You wouldn't be here to help me if you couldn't come with me! Just put your toes in to start! Come on! I want to see what your clothes will turn into!"

Kerka just shook her head.

The maidens and I splashed around, showing her how safe the water was. I pulled myself out of the water to talk to Kerka. I was wearing my T-shirt and jeans again, dry as a bone, as I came out of the water. To experiment, I lowered back into the water. Instantly I was all slick green wet suit and flippers. I got out again—jeans and T-shirt! Cool!

Kerka hadn't even noticed my transformation. Instead, she was pacing back and forth at the edge of the pond, having a conversation with herself. "I can handle a Kalis stick. I can play soccer. I can sail. I can skate. I'm just afraid to go underwater. But there is *no reason* to be afraid."

I went up to her and touched her arm. She looked at me with a frustrated expression.

"It's okay. I'll help you," I said, remembering how Dad was when he took me to swim classes back home in Califa. "We'll just take this slowly, and I'll be with you."

Kerka nodded and lifted her chin. She strode back to the edge of the water. "I can do this!" she announced. But then she stood there, continuing her argument with herself. "I can't. Yes, I can! I can't. But I will do this, I will!"

I waited, giving her a little time to gather her courage—before I would push her in myself. I knew she'd be okay with the river maidens. Getting in was the scariest part. Once that was done, Kerka would be fine!

Then, without warning, the maidens reached up and touched Kerka's arms. Just like me, she fell instantly into the pond. But unlike me, she thrashed around (in a shimmering amethyst wet suit). She disappeared beneath the surface, then her head came up again.

"Birdie!" she yelped before her head went back under.

I jumped in and started swimming toward her. Why weren't the maidens helping her? Where were they?

Then I saw them under the water with Kerka. They were pulling her down!

Kerka popped up one last time, arms thrashing, her eyes huge and panicky. Then she went under, and I couldn't see her or the river maidens anywhere, only ripples on the surface of the water where Kerka had been.

"Kerka!" I screamed as I swam to the spot where she had disappeared.

I dove beneath the water, opening my eyes to look for Kerka. What were the maidens trying to do? Drown her? Maybe that old Finnish legend was actually true!

The water was a misty green, and where the land was, it looked like a wall of rock that went down farther than I could see. I could just make out Kerka struggling with the river maidens a ways below me. I swam down, the suit and fins making me as fast as a seal. Before I reached Kerka, though, my lungs started burning. I turned, ready to rise to the surface for another breath when something grabbed my ankles!

5

The Underwater Journey

I looked down. It was one of the river maidens. She smiled at me and nodded. I shook my head frantically, trying to get away. The river maiden looked frustrated. Then she let go of one of my ankles, touched her nose, and made a sound almost like breathing. I was so surprised that I didn't try to get away again; instead, I just said "What?" The word came out almost clearly, with just a hint of a gurgle.

As soon as I said that one word, I was breathing. I laughed, and drew in a great big breath. I could breathe underwater, just like a fish! I was a fish girl—and a shiny green one, at that. I would have tumbled around like an otter to celebrate, but I had a friend to save.

"I'm here, Kerka!" I shouted, trying to get my

bearings again. My voice traveled loudly through the water.

The river maiden pointed down. Below us, I could see the two maidens surrounding a limp Kerka. I swam down as fast as I could. Kerka's eyes were open and bulging. She had stopped struggling to save energy, and now she was just holding her breath.

"You can breathe!" I said. "All you have to do is breathe, just like on land, Kerka!"

Kerka looked stubborn, even as she was about to pass out. But she couldn't very well argue with me, as I was breathing and talking underwater myself. She closed her eyes and took in a big gulp of water. She opened her eyes, and bubbles came from her mouth as she exhaled. Then a smile spread across her face. "I *can* breathe!" Kerka said. "And talk!"

"Cool, huh?" I said, bubbling back. "The river maidens only pulled you under to make you breathe so you'd feel okay with swimming underwater."

The river maidens giggled happily. Kerka giggled, too, and started floating around like a sleek amethyst angel. "If only I'd known," she said, "I wouldn't have struggled. In fact, I would have jumped in ages ago!"

"Well," I said, "communication doesn't seem to

be the river maidens' best skill. They did what they could."

The river maidens gurgled their approval as they watched Kerka start swimming as if she were born to it.

Just then, two weird things happened. First, I heard a tiny voice say, *"Fortis!"* (*Fortis* is Latin for "Bravo! Nice job!") I circled around to see where the voice had come from. The voice called again. I swam toward the rock wall, and it came into focus through the misty water. A large red flower was sprouting from a crevice, waving its head back and forth in the mild current. I had never seen or read about that kind of flower before. But we were in a magical dream world, so likely it was some sort of magic flower, maybe even a talking one.

"Did you just say 'Bravo'?" I asked it, in Latin. Well, my Latin tenses weren't quite *that* advanced, so what I said was something more like "You say 'Bravo'?"

"Fortis!" the flower said again, its voice sweet and clear.

A strange underwater flower was talking! Speaking Latin! To me!

"Hey, Kerka!" I cried out. "This flower is talking,

and I am talking back! I wish my mom could be here to see this!"

But the *second* thing that had happened was keeping Kerka entertained. The maidens were tossing a big bubble back and forth like a transparent beach ball. Inside the bubble were Kerka's backpack and her Kalis stick!

"I guess my equipment's in good hands," Kerka said with a smile.

The maidens all dove, like synchronized swimmers, taking the bubble with them.

Kerka and I exchanged hesitant looks.

"I guess this is it," I said. "Time to go!"

Kerka nodded. "I'm ready!"

I shouted "Good-bye!" (*"Bonus!"*) to the red flower before we dipped toward the darkness at the bottom of the river. Kerka and I followed the sound of the maidens' musical voices.

"I like swimming like this," I said.

"It's like we were given gills," Kerka agreed.

The thought of gilled girls made me giggle for some reason. A bouquet of shiny bubbles came from my mouth and sped toward the surface.

"By the way," Kerka said then, swimming closer to me, "what did you say back there? Something about wishing your mother could see you?"

I didn't even know Kerka had heard me! I searched for a reason for my Mom comment. A straightforward reason was that my mother had made me take Latin on Saturdays for the last two years (don't ask why), and I think this was the first time I'd ever actually spoken it in real life (does a dream world count as real life?). Anyway, the other reason was that I wanted my mother to be happy for me, but I didn't know if she actually could. You know how some moms always know the right thing to say to their kid? My mom wasn't one of them. I mean, she was great in some ways (she liked to take me shopping, and she made a killer potato salad!), but my dad was the one I always went to for understanding. I did have a few memories of my mom being different, a long time ago, when I was really little.

"Birdie, I get the feeling that you and your mother have nothing in common," Kerka said, rewinding her braid as she kicked ahead.

"We don't," I said frankly. As we swam deeper, the turquoise waters were growing darker, turning more cobalt blue. Up ahead, where we would soon be swimming, it looked dark as night. "Creepy, isn't it?" I said.

"Creepy about not getting along with your

mom? Or creepy about swimming into that darkness?" she asked.

"The darkness," I said.

"Oh." Kerka was quiet for a moment. "But about your mom," she began again. (Obviously, she wasn't going to let me off the hook.) "Could it be because you carry a part of her in you—like we each carry a part of our parents? Maybe you're afraid you'll become her?"

"I don't know," I said, thinking of how my mom turned her back on Mo, how it was more important for her to understand the people she worked with than to understand me. My mom had no idea about my hopes, my dreams. I wriggled my legs, shooting myself ahead in the direction of the maidens.

"Birdie?" Kerka caught up with me and waved her hand in front of my face, like I'd checked out of the conversation. "Do you resemble your mom? Or the other women in your family?"

"I don't know," I said again. "I guess I have Mom's eyes. I look kind of like Mo, in my coloring. But I don't remember my dad's mom, since she died when I was two."

"I don't mean physical resemblance," Kerka said, rolling her eyes. "Are you like them in spirit, the way you act?"

"Well, now that I've met her, I see I'm a lot like Granny Mo!" I said. It made me happy to know that, I realized. "My dad says Mo and Mom are like matches and gasoline together. Combustible. Mom calls Mo a crazy old bat, full of hocus-pocus. So far, Mo hasn't really said anything about Mom, at least not about the way she is now."

The walls of rock were now on all sides, as if we were in a vertical tunnel. The water had turned a darker blue, and it was getting harder to see the river maidens' watercolor tails as they swam down ahead of us. What was left of the light from the surface reflected off the bubble holding Kerka's belongings as the maidens tossed it back and forth.

"And what about *your* mom, Kerka?" I asked. I figured it was okay to ask her, now that I'd shared some of my own family . . . issues.

"I'm sorry, Birdie," she said, her voice very soft. "I'm just not really ready to talk about it. Is that all right?"

"Of course," I said. Now I felt bad that I'd asked, trying to make things even. "Even" shouldn't count between friends.

"I *do* have an older sister and a younger sister," Kerka offered, clearly feeling bad herself for not sharing—because isn't that what friends do? "I guess

I am a little like both of them, but in different ways. And I fight with my older sister sometimes, but mostly she doesn't pay attention to me. And I get along with my dad the way that you do."

It was incredibly dark and misty ahead of us, and the rock walls had gotten a lot closer. "Whoa," I said. "I wonder if the river maidens have lights or anything."

A few bubbles rose from the wall nearest us, racing to the surface that was very far away now.

Kerka grabbed my arm, and I stopped swimming immediately.

"Do you see all the eyes?" Kerka whispered in my ear.

I grabbed her hand when I saw what she was talking about. Those were eyes, sure enough, looking out through what must be crevices in the rocks: tiny glowing yellow eyes, lots of them!

"Let's catch up to the river maidens," I whispered. "And fast!"

"I knew I didn't like the water for a reason," Kerka whispered.

I gave a limp grin that no one could see. Then I squeezed Kerka's hand, and she squeezed back. Together we kicked like mad and shot downward. I couldn't see the maidens at all, but with the rock wall so close, there was only one direction they could have gone.

All at once the tunnel was filled with an eerie orange light. I glanced back. The glowing eyes had separated from the wall. They *all* belonged to a huge eel-like creature. A glowing orange ball dangled in front of the creature's wide-open mouth like a lantern. I couldn't tell if the ball was connected to its back or head or if it was some kind of monster magic.

At least we can see what's going to eat us, I thought.

Thankfully, the eel thing wasn't moving very fast. But its mouth was full of what looked like extremely sharp teeth.

Kerka turned to me, saying, "Why are you slowing down?"

"I just want to get a good look at it," I replied. "And it is moving pretty slowly."

"The only kind of predator that moves slowly is one that knows it will be catching its dinner," said Kerka.

I gulped, and decided we needed help, just as the eel shot some kind of light dart at us. I didn't wait to find out what it was. "Come on Kerka, let's book."

We both put on speed, kicking our flippers as fast as we could. While more of the eel's light darts shot at us, I screamed to the river maidens ahead of us, my voice echoing through the tunnel. "Hey! There's a giant river monster back here!"

As soon as they heard me, the maidens spun around and shot back through the water. They circled around Kerka and me, moving in a watery blur of protection. Through their protective circle, we could see glowing darts shooting from the giant eel's many eyes. They looked electrical somehow—like they would stun or shock you, and then the monster would gobble you up.

One of the river maidens gave a high-pitched shriek. A dart must have gotten her! The other two maidens immediately gathered up their limp companion and swam off quickly, the injured maiden's hair flowing behind them. We didn't even have a chance to say good-bye, and, honestly, I didn't even think about it, because now we had this big monster to deal with—alone!

Kerka and I swam and dodged darts as if we were in a living video game. Luckily, the creature was not exactly aiming. In a particularly bright blast of darts, I saw what looked like a small opening in the tunnel wall.

"Cave in the wall," I told Kerka breathlessly.

She looked hastily. "I think I see it. Let's work our way over there."

Crazily dodging the light darts, we finally made it to the little cave and squeezed in together. We barely fit. The darts were whizzing past us. Now I noticed that they made a weird whistling sound in the water. We waited until there was a lot less of the whistling going past us. Finally, the lights petered out altogether, and we were left in the dark.

"I don't think it's very smart," whispered Kerka. "Predators for whom game is plentiful don't have to be clever."

I shuddered, thinking of Kerka and me as "game," but I saw what she meant. "Let's wait a little longer," I whispered back.

The wait felt like a long one, but it was probably only five minutes. Everything was silent. We peeked out into the darkness.

"How can we tell if it's gone?" I asked Kerka.

"We can't—we just have to risk it," she answered. "I'll go first."

"Really?" I asked. "That would be great."

"Here I go," Kerka said.

I felt her moving out of our little shelter and instantly felt like a coward. If there was something to face, we should face it together. I took a deep breath and swam out a little. I saw a tiny bit of dim light approaching us.

"What's that?" I asked.

Kerka laughed. "It's my bubble with all my gear in it. The maidens must have dropped it."

"I didn't realize it had that glow to it before," I said.

"Me neither," said Kerka. "But let's get it and get out of here! And keep a look out for anything else that looks hungry or dangerous."

We swam down to the bubble and pushed it in front of us, making sure to keep an eye out in all directions. That was clearly the smart thing to do, but it meant we really couldn't talk. The tunnel flattened out and then began going up again. It grew wider and wider, and finally we saw a sparkling light up ahead. The light got brighter and the walls receded until we were in clear blue water with silvery little fish darting everywhere. Then we were swimming along a shallower area, not swimming upward at all. The river floor was carpeted with thick mossy grass, water lilies floated above our heads, and sparkling light dappled everything.

One of the river maidens swam toward us, and I saw the other two behind her (whichever one had been hit by the light dart was clearly okay now). The river maidens laughed and swam about, changing colors as if one of them hadn't just been hurt and they hadn't abandoned us. I looked over at Kerka. She shrugged, and I laughed as we followed the maidens while they poked their heads above the waterline.

The maidens pulled themselves up on some rocks that formed the wall of a little natural pool, and stretched their bodies out in the sunlight. As Kerka and I climbed up with considerably less grace, our regular clothes instantly reappeared on us (bone dry!). We both flopped onto the warm rocks and sighed in relief. From that position, I spotted a beautiful flower bush nestled in the rocks just below the surface of the little pool. I immediately recognized it. The flower stems were long and vinelike and floated in the water.

"Kerka, there they are! Our Agminium!" The flowers hummed and murmured among themselves as they shyly pushed their pink blossoms to the surface.

"*Pulchritudo. Bellus. Formosus,*" they said in unison as they emerged to greet us.

I blinked and grinned. "Wow . . . They're speaking Latin, too!"

I bowed to them and said, "*Salutatio.*"

Suddenly the river maidens all leapt into the water again. They splashed at the rocky edge of the pond and sang and giggled in delight. Then they stared at Kerka and me and put out their hands, palms down. It took some sign language before we realized that we were supposed to kiss their hands in thanks.

"A little dramatic?" Kerka whispered to me, grinning.

"Very," I agreed.

But we decided to oblige the river maidens anyway. After all, we had arrived safe and sound. With a great deal of ceremony, we slipped into the water and swam to the maidens. We kissed each of their hands, nodding our heads and batting our eyelashes as much as possible. They batted their eyelashes back at us and turned color after color, giving us one final light show before they swam away.

Kerka and I climbed out of the river again at the little pool where the Agminium flowers lived. Many of the flowers had poked their heads up out of the water.

"Ave, amica," the flowers said, speaking in a chorus and swaying as if there were a breeze in the water.

I laughed and turned to Kerka. "This is amazing!" Then I went back to the pink-petaled family. "Friend flowers, can you show us the way to the fairies?" I asked in the best Latin I could muster.

They gave me an ensemble nod. But first, it seemed, they were anxious to tell us a story. Here's my translation of it:

One beautiful day the Agminium heard a loud crash. They looked up from beneath the water to see that a shimmering stone had hit the rocks and broken in two: One half fell to the ground, and the other half dropped to the edge of their pond. A walking human shadow picked up the stone from the ground and disappeared. Then the flowers hid their heads as a flying shadow dove from the sky. The shadow snatched the broken piece from the shallow water and disappeared into the sky. Ever since that day, the special tree of Aventurine has been slowly dying. The land near the tree is dark, and the plants near it are dying as the shadow spreads. The fairies do not know how or when it is to be stopped, for they cannot change something that has a human beginning. They can only wait, as do the Agminium.

I pulled the Singing Stone from my pocket. It hummed in my hand. "Was this one half of the stone you saw?" I asked, holding it out for the flowers to see.

"Yes," they chorused. "We recognize its song and its light."

"Do you know where the other half is?" I asked.

They sadly shook their pink heads. "It is gone, taken by the flying shadow."

"I think the other half is still here in Aventurine," I told them. "This half was kept safe in my world."

Kerka nudged me. "The fairies? Remember?"

"Oh, right!" I said. Then I asked the flowers as politely as I could, in Latin, how to find the fairies.

The flowers swayed. "There is an apple tree that way," they said, their pink petals dipping in one direction. Kerka and I turned to see where they were pointing. "Start there, and go through the Orchards of Allfruit. Just past there is the Lilac Wall that protects the home of the Willowood Fairies."

"Thank you," I said. "But what is allfruit? How will we know the orchard?"

"An orchard is an orchard and allfruit is allfruit," the flowers added, ducking back under the water one by one. The pond sparkled and blurred where the flowers had gone down.

"Come on, let's get to the apple tree and find the orchard and the fairies," said Kerka.

The maidens had put Kerka's pack and stick on the rocks, so she was all set to go. I wanted to stop and think about what the flowers had said, but Kerka just wasn't made that way, so off we went at a quick pace. It took us all of two minutes to find the apple tree, whose branches were full of shiny red apples. I picked two of them while Kerka was looking around.

"Here, Kerka," I said, tossing her an apple.

It didn't surprise me one bit when she caught it easily in one hand.

"Oh, cool!" I said, taking a crunchy bite. Sweet juice dripped down my chin. "Do you see that, Kerka?" I pointed to the marigolds and garlic that grew in neat circles around the apple tree.

"I see flowers and some other plant," Kerka replied, eating her apple. "What's the big deal?"

"It's called companion planting. The flowers are marigolds, and they keep away beetles. The other plant is garlic, which keeps disease from the tree. My dad taught me that in our garden in Califa. He's a bit of a botanist, too, like my granny Mo."

"Neat," said Kerka. "Hey, Birdie, doesn't your mom teach you *anything*?"

I sighed. This girl was not going to let go of the mom thing. "Well, my mom isn't the Mother Earth type. She's all about business. Making money. Working long hours, you know? I guess she could teach me about that if I was interested." I thought I'd turn the conversation over to her. "I'm really sorry about *your* mom," I said gently. "Was she a gardener?"

Kerka shot me a weird look. "You *really* don't like her, do you, Birdie? Your mom, I mean."

Obviously, neither of us wanted to talk about her mother, so I changed the subject altogether. "So, where're these Orchards of Allfruit, do you think?" I asked.

"That way," Kerka said, pointing across the grassy field that was beyond the apple tree we were under.

"Oh yeah," I said. "I see it, I think." There were definitely trees, and they seemed to be laid out in rows, so Kerka was probably right.

"Let's go!" said Kerka.

Boy, could that girl march along! It was as if she were going to battle, or maybe going to kick a ball really hard. I had a great time *not* marching but flitting about like a butterfly as I saw interesting little wildflowers hidden all the way across the field. Even the Agminium flowers' words about things not being as they seemed didn't matter here. After all, there were a lot of things in my life that weren't as they seemed, right? Mo seemed kooky, but she was totally sane—obviously fairies and dream worlds were real. And my mom seemed sane to anyone but me, and I knew she was crazy. See what I mean?

Anyway, we reached the orchard (it was definitely an orchard up close). "More apple trees!" I exclaimed. "I guess the allfruit must be farther in." I peered into the orchard; it went on and on as far as I could see. I was standing there just goggling at what appeared to be miles of trees when Kerka walked past me.

"What are you waiting for, Birdie?" she called back to me. "We've got places to go, fairies to see! Are you always this slow?"

"I *am* always this slow!" I told Kerka when I had caught up with her. "At least when there are lots of plants around. Are you always this fast?"

"Yes," she answered as we began walking together, or rather, she strode and I kind of skipped. "At least when there's somewhere to go. I guess I don't like sitting still that much."

"And I love sitting, well, not sitting, but not marching all around like you," I said. "Gardening is like being in action but all in one place. Unless you have to carry a lot of soil from one spot to another."

We kept chatting as we walked through the apple trees. Until I noticed that they weren't apple trees anymore but pear trees. I pointed to a ripe pear. "The apple orchard just became a pear orchard," I said.

"At least we won't go hungry," said Kerka, picking a pear.

I picked one, too. It was as delicious as the apple had been.

The pear trees became peach trees, and a little bell went off in my head. "I bet *this* is what the Agminium meant by allfruit!" I said. "So the trees will be all different kinds of fruit. Cool!" I looked along the row of peach trees where we were walking, then back to where we had just been. I couldn't see the field any longer, only fruit trees. "I wonder how many kinds of fruit there are," I said.

"If you wonder too long, all the fairies will be asleep and in their beds," said Kerka. "Come on!"

"Just so you know," I added, "all these kinds of fruit trees together? Not normal."

Kerka rolled her eyes, but she smiled. We ate our way through peaches, apricots, oranges, mangoes, bananas, and olives. The sun was well past the midpoint, and my feet were starting to ache from walking when I smelled a sweet scent wafting toward us through the olive trees.

6

The Willowood Fairies

"I smell flowers," said Kerka, sounding surprised. (I guess she's not one to stop and smell the roses too often! Ha-ha.)

"That's lilac," I told her.

"So we must be coming to the Lilac Wall," said Kerka.

We continued through the olive trees, the lilac scent growing stronger every moment. Finally, we came out of the Orchards of Allfruit. Right in front of us was a wall. It was the strangest wall I'd ever seen. It was eight or nine feet tall and looked like it was made of handblown glass—you know, the kind that's not completely clear, with bubbles going through it? Right through the glass, we could see lilacs on the other side. So I guess that made it the Lilac Wall, right?

Kerka and I both touched the wall. It was cool and smooth. Kerka rapped on the wall with her knuckle. It sounded hard. I rapped on it, too: totally solid.

"Hmm," I said. "How are we going to get through that?"

"Not through," said Kerka. *"Over."*

We turned back to the little olive trees. Kerka measured them with her eyes.

"No way," I said. "They aren't close enough to the wall, plus they aren't strong enough at the top even if we found one that *was* close to the wall."

"Then we just have to walk around the wall until we find a gate or something," said Kerka.

I groaned. "Can't we take a break, pleeeeease?"

"All right," said Kerka. "But you wouldn't survive if you lived with *my* sisters. Although you kind of remind me of Biba."

I leaned on the wall and let myself slide down its cool side. "Ah," I said. "That feels great. My poor feet!" I took off my sneakers, which had never hurt my feet before in my whole life, and my socks. I wiggled my bare toes.

Kerka put her backpack on the ground and got her Kalis stick out. She started doing the graceful dance with a few leaps thrown in. *Where does she get the energy?* I wondered.

The smell of lilacs filled the air. Bees buzzed around innocently. I sighed and enjoyed the moment of peace. In the relative silence, I looked closely at Kerka's backpack for the first time. It was pretty, kind of a thick, lineny cream-colored fabric with blue and yellow embroidery of stags and mountains on it. "I love your bag," I said.

"My mom made it for me," said Kerka between leaps and stick swooshes. "I have it in the real world, too. But it didn't have my usual stuff in it when I got to Aventurine, just my Kalis stick and the map." She stopped the swooshing.

We looked at each other.

"The map!" we said at the same time.

Kerka and I scrambled for her bag, but I got there first and pulled it open and took out the map.

"Zally will know how to get in," I said.

"I bet she will," said Kerka. "Here, let me help you."

Kerka got the red string off the map, and together we unrolled it. The sun was low, its light filtering through the glass wall. We watched the map take its time to show us Zally herself, and then it filled itself in. We both stepped back while we watched it, just in case a bunch of sparks flew out of the map again.

The pictures that appeared on the map were different from the last time. Now there was a walled area surrounded by rivers and forests and ringed with mountains. The map zoomed in to the place we were now, complete with a little drawing of Kerka and me!

"We already know where we are," I told the map. "We need to get past the wall."

A shower of sparks flew up from the map. This time they were brilliant green with copper and purple bits. Slowly they formed the shape of a tree with a very long branch. The image hung there for a moment, then burst into another silent firework, showering down onto the map.

"So there's got to be a big tree along the wall," Kerka said.

"Well, it wasn't an apple tree," I said, thinking about the image. "The branch was too straight and too long to be a fruit-tree branch."

"It doesn't really matter," said Kerka. "As long as we can find it, climb it, and get over! At least we know it's along the wall somewhere." She rolled up the map and stowed it in her backpack along with the

Kalis stick. "Did you learn tree stuff from your dad, too? What, was he a farmer in . . . what did you call it? Califa?"

"Nuh-uh," I said, putting my socks and sneakers back on. "We just had a big backyard. And I read a lot. You know, books about nature, botany, plants, that sort of thing."

Kerka shook her head. "Not something I'd ever read!"

"We're different, all right!" I said.

"Yeah," Kerka said. She glanced along the glass wall in either direction. "You have climbed trees before, haven't you?" she asked, looking at me a little doubtfully.

"I'm not, like, super sport girl," I said. "But I can climb trees!"

"Okay, tree lover, which direction should we look for this big tree that will get us over the wall?" Kerka asked with a grin.

Now it was my turn to glance to the right and the left along the length of the wall. It curved away from us in either direction, and I couldn't see any sign of a big tree. I closed my eyes and tried to *feel* a big tree. I turned my head from side to side. The smell of lilacs was stronger in one direction. I didn't know if that meant anything, but it was better than nothing.

I opened my eyes. "That way," I said, pointing to the left.

"All right, then," said Kerka. "We're off to find a tree!"

As we walked, I told Kerka about all the kinds of trees I thought it might or might not be. I don't usually talk so much, but Kerka seemed to be listening, and it was one of my favorite topics. The Orchards of Allfruit were on our left side (they really were big!), and the glass wall with the lilacs behind it was on our right side. Neither view changed, although the sun was sinking lower.

"I don't think that was a willow tree," I was saying when we saw the tree we were looking for.

It was a Hybrid Oak, a cross between a *Quercus* (like the Glimmer Tree) and a *hawkinsi*. I'd just seen one like it with my mom at the Brooklyn Botanic Garden, one of the few places I really loved in New York City. I shared my knowledge with Kerka, who listened with good humor. (I think she was really getting used to me!)

"That's so cool, Birdie," she said. "Now, can we climb it and get over the wall?"

I grinned and nodded. "Let's do it."

The branches of the oak hung along the wall and stretched over a sea of lilac bushes—just like the image out of the map. Kerka bowed and waved her hand for me to go first. So I did, scrambling up the bottom branches. Kerka came behind me, climbing like a cat.

I got to the big branch that went out over the wall. I sat on it and inched myself forward bit by bit. It was a long way down! To give Kerka credit, she didn't tell me to go faster. She walked along the branch behind me like a tightrope walker. The branch angled slightly down after it went over the glass wall, thankfully!

"Hold on to the branch and lower yourself down from there," Kerka suggested.

So that's what I did, a little clumsily and holding my breath. With a *thump* I dropped into the lilac bushes. Kerka landed beside me with no *thump* whatsoever.

We pushed our way through the tall lilacs and came out in a blue flower garden. Seriously—every plant was blue! There were blue spires, wisteria, blue irises, bluebonnets, blue chrysanthemums, delphiniums, and bluebells. I had never seen so many shades of blue all in one place!

"Is this the most beautiful, incredible, magical flower garden you've ever seen?" I said to Kerka. "It's even more amazing than Mo's garden." I stood breathing in the scents. The sweet lilacs mixed with a cool smell of spearmint and hyacinth and blue rose.

Kerka was actually impressed, too. She gazed around. "I've never seen anything like it!"

Together we tiptoed through the flowers to a path of polished glass shards that twisted through the garden. I was suddenly hit by a memory of my mother—a good one.

Years ago she had taken me to a playground. She wore jeans and slid down the curlicue slide with me, over and over, as many times as I wanted. Then we lay on a blanket in the grass and watched the clouds. My mother pointed to a flower-shaped cloud in the sky. "See the flower?" she asked me. "It's a daisy, turning toward the sun."

"That cloud *did* look like a daisy, didn't it?" said a voice.

Kerka and I spun around. What was it about this place and voices coming out of nowhere? I almost laughed, but the sight of the woman gliding down the glass path through the blue garden stopped the sound from coming up. Instead, I gave a little gulp.

Bees buzzed like banjo strings around the lady in the late-afternoon sunlight. Her dress was turquoise, and white spider lilies adorned the hem and dotted her upswept hair. "Put that away," she said sternly.

I gaped, not knowing what she was talking about but wanting to do whatever she asked. I thought she looked like the spider lilies on her dress—*Amaryillidaceae lycoris.*

"Sorry, just a reflex," Kerka said. Out of the corner of my eye, I saw her slowly putting the Kalis stick back in her pack. She must have whipped it out in surprise at the woman's voice. I almost giggled again to see Kerka look so meek.

"You don't need the Kalis stick here," said the spider lily woman. "Not unless you are dancing."

I pressed my lips together tightly to keep the giggles down. This woman was like the coolest, strictest teacher in my old school—but definitely stranger!

"When you visit the Willowood Fairies, you are under our protection," the woman continued, with her sweet smile and steely tone. I finally looked past the buzzing bees and noticed her wings. How could I have missed them? They were huge, and the lightest iridescent blue.

"Come with me, Birdie," she said, the huge wings folding like a butterfly's as she walked away from us. "Kerka, too!"

"Okay, but who are you?" I asked, following, my eyes on her wings.

The fairy queen turned to answer; her gossamer wings and glistening dress made a swishing sound. "I'm Patchouli, the Queen of the Willowood Fairies. Come quickly, now."

Queen Patchouli led us out of the blue garden onto a path of stones carved like leaves. This path went right into a weeping willow woods that I hadn't even noticed because the blue garden was so awesome. We walked between the trees until the queen stopped and pulled aside layers of soft leaf-filled branches on a huge willow tree. She motioned for us to follow her inside.

Under the tree's shelter was a cozy room draped with white gauzy curtains that let in the light. Music traveled on the breeze and rustled the streaming willow branches. "It's time for you both to choose proper attire," Queen Patchouli said.

I exchanged a look with Kerka, who did her usual shrug. Then I saw my very own suitcase sitting on the ground, but with one new detail. A shining gold *A* glistened on the front, in the same script as had been on Mo's *Aventurine* violin case. I looked inquisitively at Queen Patchouli (who, in my head, I was now calling Queen P.).

"What is my suitcase doing here?" I asked.

"It has your clothes in it," the fairy queen said. She flicked her hands toward the suitcase. Her fingers tinkled; she was wearing rings with tiny bells on them! "Go ahead. Open it!"

I opened the latches and felt a rumble as the entire bag began to shake. I stepped back. The suitcase turned inside out, rose up like a stretched accordion, and slowly became a ten-foot-tall wooden wardrobe. An old woman's face was carved at the top, wreathed with flowers.

"I was only staying at Mo's for three days," I joked. "I certainly didn't pack all *that*!"

I inched toward the large wardrobe. The sides were covered in the same stickers as my old suitcase. The fairy queen pulled open the wardrobe doors. It was packed with clothes, and mirrors hung on the inside of each door. Kerka came up beside me to look in as well.

"Go on," the fairy queen urged.

"Dress for adventure." She looked from Kerka to me. "And don't worry, the clothes are all fairy-made, so they will fit both of you."

Kerka and I riffled through colorful dresses, silk saris, suede ponchos, satin kimonos, velvet jackets, and gypsy skirts hanging on the racks. My favorites were a cloak trimmed in golden beads like berries, a cotton sarong embroidered with fall leaves, and a skirt of peacock feathers. There was every fabric I'd ever seen hanging there, plus some that were unfamiliar and felt like water or cobwebs.

We opened a huge bottom drawer to find more: knobby-knit sweaters, patched jeans, woolly tights, and patterned leggings. On a top shelf was more footwear than it seemed possible to hold, everything from galoshes and glittered shoes to cowboy boots and tap shoes. The queen showed us one more drawer, which telescoped out to display masks, fairy wings, necklaces, tiaras, bangles and bracelets, paper fans, scarves of every shape and size, and hats with ribbons and feathers in every color of the rainbow.

"So, dress for adventure, right?" I said to the fairy queen.

"Adventure, danger, whatever you want to call it," said the queen. "You'll do wonderfully, but don't take too long!" With that, she swept out of our dressing-room bower.

"Come on, Kerka, let's do wonderfully!" I said.

We dug into the clothes like pirates dive into a treasure chest. I picked a pair of boots much like Mo's but with glittery green laces.

"What do you think?" I asked, lacing them up.

"Definitely, yes!" said Kerka. "Fun but practical."

"Well?" Kerka asked. I turned and saw that her eyes and nose were covered by a sequined bird mask.

"Absolutely not!" I declared. "Too much of a disguise."

I chose a spring green tunic stitched with daisies that reminded me of Belle, and a long lacy white skirt. "How about this?" I asked, twirling so the lace of the skirt floated up.

Kerka frowned.

"No on the skirt, huh?" I said. I hung it back up and pulled on sky-blue velvet cargo pants instead. They had deep pockets into which I put my half of the Singing Stone. Then I tied an eggplant-purple kerchief on my head like a headband. When I saw the carved-wood wardrobe lady wink, I knew I looked good. But what I liked about the outfit was how the daisies on the shirt reminded me of Belle, how the color of the scarf reminded me of Mo's house, and how the color of the pants reminded me of my old blue door back in Califa.

I checked myself out in the mirror. The purple scarf brought out the gold highlights in my hair. *Red-bird, looks like your hair's on fire!* I said to myself, remembering what my dad used to tell me when my hair shone in the sunlight. I smiled; even my braces didn't bother me in this outfit. Finally, I threw a bright green velvet cloak over my shoulders.

Kerka came up beside me to look in the mirror. She had on nut-brown leggings and a tunic similar to the one I'd chosen except in a golden-brown color. Over the tunic, she had on a long medieval-looking brocade vest in night-sky blue, with a snow leopard embroidered on it in silver thread that wrapped from the front to the back. Her over-the-knee boots were dark blue suede with more stars.

"You look great!" I said. "Like a girl knight or something."

"Why, thank you," she answered, putting her nose in the air and holding her Kalis stick like it was a sword.

We heard a tiny bell ring.

"Are you ready?" Queen Patchouli called.

"We are!" Kerka and I replied together.

Kerka put on her backpack. Then we shut the

wardrobe doors carefully. As soon as we did, the whole thing folded itself back up, one side at a time, *bam ka-bam,* until all that sat on the floor was my vintage suitcase. With a *clip, clip,* it snapped itself shut. Laughing at the wonderful magic show, Kerka and I walked out through the wispy willow branches.

The queen wasn't there, but underfoot was a fresh path of yellow and orange flower petals that released their scent as we stepped on them. We walked over the petals through feathery willow trees toward the sound of voices and music. Finally, we pushed aside the branches of one last tree and stepped into a giant clearing that was a perfect circle. The sun was setting, spreading deep golden light across the whole amazing scene.

The place was filled with fairies. None of them was small, as I had imagined fairies would be. They were the size of humans—like Queen Patchouli. They all had gauzy wings and gorgeous outfits. Every one of them wore flowers, either tucked behind their ears, or woven into crowns, or as buttons up and down their clothes.

The fairies were busy, setting tables that were placed in concentric circles. The tables were piled with food and flowers. It was like being at a wedding for a movie star who was crazy about fairies.

Suddenly I felt eyes on me, and I noticed that many of the fairies were staring at me as they went past, carrying trays of food, or piles of silken napkins, or baskets of silverware.

Then Queen P. was beside us. "There you are!" she said. "Just in time. Come along." As she walked through the fairy crowd, her people parted before her like waves.

I saw that Kerka had her own fan club of fairies watching her and whispering as we passed.

The queen led us to a small table in the center of the fairy ring that was on a raised circle of earth covered in growing grass. She went up the grassy steps to the round table, motioning for us to follow. There were only three chairs at the table, two woven of willow branches, for Kerka and myself, and a bigger willow chair festooned with roses that was clearly for the queen.

As we sat, Queen Patchouli rang a small glass bell. A delicate but piercing sound filled the air. The fairies went silent and all quickly found a seat at one of the tables around the circle.

"Now, this is Birdie Cramer Bright," Queen Patchouli announced. "And Kerka Laine. This is the beginning of Birdie's fairy godmother training and a little of Kerka's, but her own quest is for another time."

"Are you all fairy godmothers?" I blurted out, my curiosity having got the best of me.

"Heavens, no!" said the queen. "Fairy godmothers are human. We fairies have never been human and never can be." Did I imagine it, or did a ripple of regret pass through the fairies? "We personally know all of the fairy godmothers, of course," Queen P. went on. "And all of the fairy-godmothers-in-the-making."

"So I'm going to be a fairy godmother?" I asked. "And Kerka?"

"Maybe you will be a fairy godmother, maybe not," said Queen P. "We'll see how you handle your first and most important quest. There are things you have to learn to become a fairy godmother. Things about yourself, other people, the way the world can be changed."

I must have rolled my eyes, because the queen stopped and looked at me sternly. "I know that this sounds like lessons to you, but consider that anything you do, anything at all, makes you learn and discover. Do not underestimate the power of experience, Birdie Cramer Bright."

The queen's intensity was a little scary. I took a

deep breath and nodded. It was so strange that I couldn't quite believe it was happening to me. I hoped I was up for whatever was next.

"May I ask a question?" I asked.

"You just did," said Queen P. "But yes, ask a question."

"If I become a fairy godmother, what will I do? Do I have to, like, find someone like Cinderella and help her?"

The fairies all broke out in laughter. I could feel my cheeks getting red. Queen P. finally had to ring her bell again to get the fairies to stop. Then she said, "Birdie is not completely wrong. Fairy godmothers *do* help people." She turned to me. "But the people you will help won't always know what you are doing. You will have a magic in your world that can make a difference, not just to people but also to the world itself. And in your case, your family—those of the Arbor Lineage—has magic that helps the green world the most."

"Oh," I said. I didn't really know what to say. I hoped that Mo would be able to help me understand exactly what I was supposed to do back home, assuming I succeeded in this quest. I looked at Kerka; she shrugged at me (which seemed to be her answer to everything).

The queen put a hand on each of our heads for a moment and smiled down at us. Then she took her hands away and waved them at the fairies. "Now let us eat, fairies of Willowood and fairy-godmothers-to-be—the night is just beginning."

7

The Book of Dreams

The sun had set when we finished eating the amazing meal. (I wished that I hadn't had all that fruit on the way there!) I had never eaten so much in my life and was feeling a little sleepy. Kerka and I talked to the fairy queen about our families . . . well, mostly *I* talked, for once.

When the last of the glass plates was cleared, the queen rang the little bell again, and silence fell. From beneath the blossoms of a lone magnolia tree to one side of the fairy ring, a fairy all dressed in spring green approached, holding something bulky—it was *The Book of Dreams*! Rose and lilac petals fell like snow as she headed toward us and handed the book to Queen Patchouli. The book was as yellowed and tattered and mysterious as it had been when it appeared on my mom's old bed.

"Let us begin, shall we?" said Patchouli, laying both hands on the book. "Everyone close your eyes, except Birdie. You too, Kerka." Patchouli lifted her hands from the front cover, and the book opened by itself, flipping page after page until it stopped. "Here we are. Emma's dream," she said as she slid the book over to me.

My mother? I thought in amazement.

"She wrote this many years ago," said the fairy queen, as if she'd heard my question. "It will begin your understanding of why you are here and what you must do."

Queen P. rang the glass bell, and as the sound rang out, a shimmering lavender mist gathered over Kerka and the fairies. I smelled lilacs.

I looked down to see my mother's own hand-writing on the page of the book, but it was curlier, more artistic, as if she had been experimenting with calligraphy and enjoying the shape of every letter.

"Read, Birdie," Queen Patchouli said.

And I did.

November 11, 1977

I am like a seedling frozen in time and waiting to break out and be a flower ... someday. I hold the family talisman stone in the palm of my hand tonight, and I know it isn't for me. I cannot fulfill the dream of my mother.

I have my own dreams now.

Aventurine and the Arbor Lineage will have to wait for another girl.

Emma

My heart ached for the girl who was now my mother. I actually understood what she'd been feeling. "What did she decide?" I asked in a whisper. "What did she do?"

The queen shook her head sadly at me and then rang the glass bell. The shimmering mist melted away. The fairies opened their eyes, nodding to each other as if they knew something now.

I looked at Kerka. She was blinking dreamily.

"I saw a page from *The Book of Dreams* in my head," Kerka said. "A girl named Emma wrote it."

"That's my mother," I said.

"Each girl who comes to Aventurine has the opportunity to make a difference here . . . and in what you call the real world," said Queen Patchouli as she gently closed the book. "Now, Birdie, you have come on your own quest."

"What exactly am I supposed to do?" I asked.

"You must find the other half of the Singing Stone, Birdie," said the fairy queen.

"Okay, I guess I can do that. Do you know where the other half of the stone is?" I asked. "The flowers said that a flying shadow took it. And what does it have to do with my mother?"

"Fairies cannot follow shadows," said Patchouli.

"All we know is that the stone piece is somewhere in Aventurine. Your mother's dream shows part of why this quest falls to you — it is your quest to find the other half of the stone and reclaim it for your family."

"And if I find it, what will happen?" I asked.

All the fairies whispered excitedly as Queen Patchouli answered, "Harmony will be restored to a part of Aventurine that has been suffering, and harmony will be restored to your family."

"And if I *don't* find it?" I asked.

All the fairies went quiet. Then Queen Patchouli said, "Then you will not have fulfilled your destiny or your family's, and it will mean terrible things for a special part of Aventurine. Terrible things for your grandmother's garden, as well. And the bonds of your family will slowly wither away."

"What?" I cried.

The fairy queen nodded, her eyes grave. "What has begun will be finished." She shook the glass bell once more.

My eyes closed heavily. Images rushed before me: the rotted spot on the Glimmer Tree, the notes dancing around on Mo's sheet music and floors and walls, my mother's journal entry.

"How did the stone break?" I asked, my eyes

still closed, hoping for a glimpse of the stone's past. I knew exactly *where* in Aventurine it had been broken, from the Agminiums' story, but I didn't know if someone had thrown it, or dropped it, or . . . ?

"How does not matter," said the queen. "What matters is that you are the only hope for the healing of the Singing Stone, the gardens, the Glimmer Tree, and your family."

"*I'm* the only hope?" I asked, pulling my velvet cloak tight.

"It is time now for you to sleep and dream," said the fairy queen. "The dreaming may help you. Or it may not. You do have some power to choose your dream as you add it to the *Book.*"

My eyes shot open. Had I been sleeping? I sat up, pushing back light cotton sheets. I was wearing a

116

spring green nightgown embroidered with daisies. This wasn't mine! I looked at the bed: It was carved with leaves and flowers and the same old woman's face that had been on the wardrobe. She smiled at me and nodded from out of the bed frame.

Clearly, I was still in Aventurine but maybe sleeping or dreaming? The fairies must have put me to bed and made bedroom walls from white curtains that hung from nothing that I could see. Above, the sky was dark as midnight, and the moon had a ring around it.

I was alone.

But something bright was flitting around my head. A firefly. It reminded me of the firefly in Dora's journal entry.

"Hello," I said. "Is this a dream now?"

The firefly stopped circling and hovered in front of my face. I gently cupped it in my hands. Its wings glistened with silvery flecks, and its little light was a phosphorescent gold.

"How am I supposed to find the other half of the stone?" I whispered. "Why am I the only hope for the Arbor Lineage to heal the green world?"

I looked around my little bedroom. A small table and chair were at the foot of the bed. On the table lay *The Book of Dreams*, the silver lettering on its cover shimmering in the moonlight.

Suddenly I felt a tingling in the center of my palm, where the firefly was. Then the golden glow from the firefly grew brighter and brighter, until it had thrown a halo around me. I got up from the carved bed and sat at the table, bathed in the firefly's light.

Now I saw that beside the book there was a peacock feather with a pointed tip—a fancy quill pen. Next to the peacock quill was a shell with a silver lid. I took off the lid and saw that the shell was filled with silver ink.

The Book of Dreams opened all by itself to a blank page.

The fairies had given me a pen and ink, a blank page, and privacy. It was my turn to write. I picked up the feather.

I wondered if Emma had sat in this very spot when she had written in the book. And perhaps Dora and Mo had, too. How far back did my family go? Had all my ancestresses sat here and written their dreams? I tried to flip through the book to check, but the pages wouldn't budge.

I sighed, and dipped the tip of the feather into the shell. I brought the tip out, and the silver ink shimmered in the moonlight. I wrote the date. It was going to be hard to write something, knowing that someday my own daughter—or granddaughter!—might read it.

I heard the breeze *whoosh-whoosh*ing through the gauze curtains. I heard *whir-whirr*ing in the willows and the firefly *buzz-buzz*ing in front of me. My mind wandered into memory.

I remembered the tree house that Mom and I built when I was little. We hammered planks onto the thick oak tree branches to make a sturdy floor that wouldn't fly off when the Santa Ana winds blew.

"Sorry, tree," we said every time we hit a nail.

"Is it okay, tree?" we'd ask, for permission.

My mom said that as long as we didn't nail too deep and we only put in the few nails that were needed, the tree would be okay. I was so happy to be in a world of our own, just me and Mom and the big oak tree. I dreaded having to come down out of that tree house to go to school, to go to bed, to go back to regular life. I wanted to stay in that tree with my mom forever.

I found myself writing, images rising unbidden to my mind. And I described them. I didn't mind that I had to dip the pen into the ink a lot. It left beautiful thick lines and slender curves, so my writing looked ancient and important. I put the pen down at the edge of the book, feeling a little strange. I closed my eyes to think. Where were these images coming from? Was I really dreaming, or was this some fairy magic?

I thought of how it felt as if Mom was deserting me when she first went back to work. Somehow her job had felt wrong to me, like she wasn't being herself. I wouldn't have minded her being away if she had been a gardener or a landscape architect. I had a vague recollection of my parents arguing about my mom's job, but I can't remember who was unhappy. Maybe they both were.

I opened my eyes. The firefly was hovering again. I picked up the feather pen and wrote.

Finally, I signed my name and set down the feather pen. I didn't want to see any more. And I thought I understood now what the dream was saying—I hoped I understood. I looked around for the fairies or the fairy queen. The firefly *whirr*ed around the book.

I looked down at the page I had just written. My writing was now illustrated with drawings of the tree and the shadow! Not only that, pressed flowers were embedded in the paper, glitter made sparkling stars among the words, and bits of satin, lace, and ribbon bordered the pages. It was beautiful.

December 31, 2008

I see a beautiful tree that glitters in the sunlight, just like my tree-house tree, just like the Glimmer Tree in Mo's garden. But this dream tree is much bigger. The dream tree drops a seed—an acorn—and it turns into stone.

The Singing Stone makes music that helps green things grow, roots reach out, and buds burst. A shadow appears and the Stone breaks. Half of it disappears into the Glimmer Tree. A flying shadow takes the other half. Now the tree is becoming a shadow itself, and so is everything around it.

My mother and Mo sit in the shadow. On the edges of the shadow is Dad. And me! The shadow is growing, both bigger and darker.

I must do something. I have to change what I see.

Birdie

I pressed my hand on my page. The firefly's glow faded. The moon was gone, and the sky was light purple.

It was time to go.

I found the opening in the curtains and walked into the fairy ring. It was empty: no tables, no fairies, nobody at all. I looked down, and I was wearing the clothes I'd chosen from the wardrobe again. I looked back. My fairy bedroom had been on the raised grassy circle where the queen's table had been. I'd sat writing all night, or at least all of a fairy night. As I watched, the white curtains disappeared into the bright rays of the rising sun that shot through the willow trees. My firefly had disappeared as well.

I thought for a moment. What did I have to do?

I had to find Kerka. Then I needed to find the Shadow Tree. I walked to the edge of the circle and was trying to figure out which of the paths to take when Queen P. came down one of them. She was wearing a bathrobe (at least, I think it was a bathrobe) of flowered velvet tied with a white satin sash; her wings somehow came out of the robe, and her hair streamed to her knees.

The fairy queen smiled and nodded at me. "It went well, I see," she said.

"I guess so," I said, not really knowing how to

THE BOOK OF DREAMS

describe the experience I'd just had. "Do you know where Kerka is?"

"Right here," said the fairy queen, waving her hand behind her.

"Birdie!" called Kerka, striding into the fairy ring. She was licking what looked like an ice cream cone and holding another one. "Breakfast!" she explained, waving a cone. "Granola cone, mango yogurt ice. I have one for you. How'd you sleep? The fairies gave me the most incredible bed—"

"Kerka!" I interrupted her. "We have to go!"

"My mother used to say that breakfast was a must," said Kerka with no sense of urgency at all. "Especially for girls who have things to do!" She held out the breakfast ice cream cone.

"She's right, breakfast is a good idea," said the fairy queen. "Plus, I need to give you something, Birdie."

The firefly was flitting around me again, shining like a jewel. "There you are, sweet gift," said Queen P., pointing to her right shoulder, where the firefly landed obediently. "Give me your hand," said the queen. "And take the light."

The fairy queen took my hand and moved it to her shoulder where the firefly sat. At once, the firefly landed on my finger. Its light moved into my finger and spread to my whole hand. The light, which glowed through my clothes, changed from pale yellow to gold as it traveled up my arm. I watched in wonder as it crept up my shoulder, turned a fiery copper, and then dropped to surround my heart.

"It's called a heart gift," the fairy queen explained. "A piece of magic from all the past fairy godmothers in your lineage is in it."

I looked over at Kerka. She had finished her breakfast while the queen had done her magic. Kerka held the other cone out to me, only dripping a little.

"Oh, all right," I said, taking it from her and smiling despite myself. Did it bother Kerka that I had gotten this amazing gift? "But we're leaving as soon as I finish it."

Luckily, Kerka didn't seem bothered or jealous at all. "Where are we going?" she asked as I licked the ice cream cone.

"To find the tree that the Agminium flowers talked about: the Shadow Tree," I said. I turned to the fairy queen. "You can point us in the right direction, can't you?"

The fairy queen nodded. "Follow me."

Kerka was like a classic heroine, striding boldly behind the queen, her bag with the Kalis stick and the map on her back. And me? I slurped on my ice cream, and I am sure I looked worried. Heart gift or no, fighting shadows, healing stones, and saving my family were not things that came easily to me.

We entered the willow woods again, walking on another glass-shard path through the trees. Then the queen led us through a garden of all orange flowers and plants over a path of crushed shells. From there we took a green moss path that went through a jungle of lilac bushes.

While we walked, Kerka told me that her pack was filled with fairy food for the journey ahead of us. I imagined that meant pastries filled with amazing fruit, or maybe some with edible flowers, like zucchini blossoms stuffed with rose petal jam. Well, that was something good to look forward to!

Of course, the lilacs were at the edge of the glass wall, which is where the moss path ended—although this was a different spot from where we'd come in. Not only lilacs pressed against the wall here, but also tall rosebushes.

The fairy queen stopped and pulled a red satin bag from her bodice. She opened the bag and pulled out two small red feathers. Then she gave one to Kerka and one to me.

I touched mine; it was like downy silk. "What are these for?" I asked.

"These are your last gift from me," said the queen with a smile.

"Thank you," I said.

Kerka smiled. "Will we be flying?" she asked.

"Something like that," said the fairy queen. "With these magic redbird feathers, you can ride the Redbird Wind."

"Is that good?" I asked.

"It will be faster than walking to the Shadow Garden," said the queen, "but it will pose challenges."

I sighed. "And I bet you won't tell us what those challenges are."

"That's right," said the queen, raising one eyebrow. "But I can tell you not to drop the feathers while you are on the wind, for their magic only works while you hold them."

I didn't say that that seemed kind of obvious to me, but Kerka and I looked at each other, and I could tell she was thinking the same thing.

As Kerka and I put our feathers into our pockets, the queen continued, "I have given you three things now: the map for direction, the heart gift for strength, and the feathers for flight. Now, here is something to remember." She reached to gently close my eyelids, and a vision from *The Book of Dreams* rose in my mind.

December 1, 1951

I am on a stage, in a spotlight, and I have to sing a song I do not know. The audience waits; I can hear their shuffling feet and impatient sighs. I want to run away, but I don't. I walk into the center of the stage, and a song just comes out. A green song, a song of green.

Then the whole room of people is singing with me. It's as if I unlocked this song inside all of them. Then I see that it isn't a theater that I am in, but a giant circle of trees. And the trees are singing, too. Then I am in a field of singing flowers, then on a wall of singing ivy, then I am back in the theater with the singing people. The theater is hung with vines of flowers and grapes and red berries, and the people wear bright masks of leaves and pansies.

Maureen

The Green Song

Don't give me diamonds
I don't need gold
Just leaves and sunlight
And a gentle wind to blow

Green
Surround and cradle me
Green
Let me breathe and sing

I can see a patch of blue
Breaking through
I can feel a little smile
Coming to me

Green
Surround and cradle me
Green
Let me breathe and sing

8

The Redbird Wind

I opened my eyes. "That was Mo's dream!" I said. "But what am I supposed to remember from it?"

"That is for you to figure out," said the fairy queen, giving Kerka and me each a kiss on the cheek. "Off you go to find the Redbird Wind."

Before I could open my mouth to ask how, Queen P. winked at us. "Just one last bit of fairy help: Follow the scent of cinnamon." She touched the glass wall, which melted away like ice, leaving enough room for both Kerka and me to walk through.

We walked into more roses and lilacs on the other side. Kerka and I each sniffed a little. Sure enough, there was the smell of cinnamon. We had to push our way through the lilacs and rosebushes to follow it. I turned around to wave to Queen P. one last time. She was gone, and I could barely make out the glass wall, whole again.

Kerka and I kept on through the bushes. Tiny thorns scratched my hands like kittens' claws until I told them to stop, in Latin. I was surprised when they did!

We emerged from the bushes into a field of wildflowers. Clearly, we were not meant to stop there, for the scent of cinnamon pulled us on. In between sniffing the air like a beautifully dressed bloodhound, I talked to the flowers.

"Ave, amicas!" I greeted them one after the other.

Soon Kerka was greeting them as well, since it was an easy phrase to pick up. We always got happy responses in return.

At the opposite side of the field was an odd rocky hill, or rather, a hill of rocks, and not just any rocks, but huge gray ones that sparkled with mica. The rocks looked as if giants had been piling them up for some purpose now long forgotten.

At the bottom of the rock hill, the breeze picked up the cinnamon smell and stirred it around.

"It smells like those tiny red Valentine candies!" I said.

"It smells like the coffee cake my mother used to make," said Kerka.

I wondered if it made her a little sad, but I didn't have time to think about that because the wind began to blow in earnest. I had to hold my fairy cloak so it wouldn't sail off. As the wind swirled up the rocky hill, it turned pink, then deepened in color until it shrouded the rocks at the top in a whirling crimson.

I leaned toward Kerka. "Do you think this is the Redbird Wind?" I asked.

Kerka gazed at the crimson wind. She nodded. "It must be. Are you ready?"

"Yes, very ready," I said. *I am going to save my family's place here in Aventurine or die trying!* I thought. Suddenly I wondered how hurt I could get in this dreamland. Wouldn't I wake up if something really bad happened? I nearly whimpered but pulled myself back together and decided not to think about it.

"Let's go to the wind, then!" Kerka said. "This'll be fun!" she added. "Didn't you always want to fly, Birdie?"

"Uh-huh," I said, trying to sound excited again. "Always."

We clambered up the rocks. I banged my knees and shins more than once, but I was determined to keep up with Kerka. We stopped before the top because that's where the red wind was now swirling like icing in motion on a cupcake. The scent of cinnamon was overwhelmingly spicy.

"Let's get out our feathers and see what happens," I suggested.

We both held our magic redbird feathers tightly in front of us. We looked around.

"I feel like we're supposed to say some magic words," I said. I giggled, thinking about how we must look: two girls in fabulous fairy clothes, holding up feathers, hoping we could fly.

Suddenly the crimson whirlwind came right at me. It pulled at my hair, which was now flying around where it wasn't held by the purple scarf. I gave a little squeak and tried to back away, but the wind pulled me toward the top of the hill. I looked over at Kerka; she had backed up and wasn't in the wind's pull.

"Help!" I shouted to her.

"Just relax and let yourself get sucked in," said Kerka. "I think that's how it's done."

"WHAT?" I shouted. "No way! That's easy for you to say—you're not the one being pulled!"

Kerka grinned. "Watch me!" she said. She headed over the rocks past me, as nimble as a mountain goat, redbird feather clutched in her hand.

What could I do? I grabbed Kerka's hand (my other hand held the feather) just in time for the wind to suck us up together.

We spun with so much force that Kerka and I were pulled apart. I shut my eyes against the stinging wind. My closed eyes calmed me, and my nose filled with the cinnamon smell. I felt the wind stop whirling. I opened my eyes, feeling a little dizzy. Below me, I could see we had gone well past the rock hill and the fairies' realm. We were flying along another river that cut through low green hills.

The wind blew, but the air was clear. The sky was an electric blue, with puffy white clouds here and there. I was in the middle of a flock of redbirds the size of crows, with long feathered tails and crests on their heads. And I was flying! I flapped my arms like wings and went faster through the air. It was like swimming in the air. It made sense that in a dreamland like Aventurine the flying was like dream flying!

I looked around for Kerka. She was gliding amidst the birds, arms outstretched, surveying the ground below.

"Kerka!" I called.

She looked over at me and grinned. "I told you it would be fun!" she called. She turned her body so that she swooped over to me.

We flew together for a while, both of us checking

out our new flying powers, our red feathers held tightly in our hands. Below us, the green hills became bigger mountains, with the turquoise river still running through them. The river crashed down in a series of magnificent waterfalls that sent spray almost all the way up to where we rode the Redbird Wind.

After the waterfalls, I zipped ahead of Kerka and the birds, right into the cool, damp center of a cloud. I could hear the birds following me, and I could see the flash of their red wings out of the corner of my eye. We burst out of the cloud back into brightness, the sun high above us.

I shot a glance behind me to see Kerka in the middle of the birds, grinning madly at me. She gave me a thumbs-up. Then I slowed down and let her catch up with me.

I was feeling deliriously happy until I spotted a patch of dark clouds far in the distance. With the sight of that cloud, it all came back to me. All I was going to have to do. All that rested on my shoulders. Below the dark clouds, the ground was shadowed in darkness. I knew I was looking at Dora's ink stain, spreading into sky, soil, tree limbs, and roots.

I turned to Kerka. "The Shadow Tree is there somewhere," I said.

"We can do it, Birdie," Kerka said, but even she

sounded a little nervous.

The dark realm came into focus as we flew on. The birds flew slower as we got closer. Below us, the mountains flattened into rocky fields and the river shrank into a stream. Then the stream shrank into a creek, the creek into a trickle, until there was nothing but rocks and weeds and dead plants. We flew slowly below the dark clouds into the cold shadow below.

I was about to ask Kerka when she thought we should land, but suddenly the redbird flock dissolved into a chaotic scramble as each bird flew in a different direction to escape the storm clouds. One of them knocked into Kerka, who struggled to stay level. I saw her redbird feather drift down just as Kerka began to fall.

I dove after her, my arms by my sides to pick up speed. When I caught up to Kerka, I wrapped my arms around her (which was hard, with the pack on her back). Instantly we both stopped falling, but with such a jerk that I nearly let go again.

"Thanks!" Kerka shouted, her voice sounding funny.

"No problem!" I said. Kerka's Kalis stick was in my face. "I can't see. It feels like we're still falling!"

"We are!" said Kerka. "Maybe if I hold the feather, too, we can share it?"

"Okay!" I answered. "Can you see it?"

"Yup!" she said. "Got it! Try letting go now."

Slowly I let go with my hand that wasn't holding the feather. Kerka didn't fall, but we were much lower than before. The wind had died, so only the magic was holding us up.

"Spread your arms," I suggested. "It should break our fall!"

For the last twenty feet or so to the ground, we spread our arms wide. My cloak caught the last of the Redbird Wind. Slowly, slowly, we spun, twirling like a giant moose wing.

Then we landed *not* so gracefully—*bam!*—right on our behinds (even Kerka).

"Whew!" I exclaimed. "That started out fun, but I'm glad it's over."

Kerka laughed and jumped to her feet. As usual, she looked around as if she were the guide. Now she nodded approvingly in each direction. "Looks safe enough to me," she announced. "Let's go, Birdie." And off she went, without looking back.

It didn't feel safe to *me*. I didn't even want to breathe in because the smell was like something old that needed a serious bath. There was a feeling of unsettling stillness, like dead air, and it seemed to seep into my skin, making my insides itchy. All around were rocks and dust and dead and dying plants. It made my heart hurt.

"The living dead," I murmured. Then I had an idea. I bent down and whispered, *"Ave, amici."*

The plants were still and silent.

I tried again, but I could tell there wasn't a chance. Any dreamland magic was gone from them, as was their life.

I sighed and stood up; the itchy-aching feeling grew worse. In the distance, the black clouds were occasionally lit by sharp jabs of lightning. Rumbles of thunder followed, and the ground shook even where we were. Kerka was already walking toward the jungle, into that dark rumbling, her clothes grayed by the dust and dirt.

"Kerka!" I called.

But she didn't turn around, and all of a sudden *she* was making me itchy and unsettled, too. She was leaving me behind as if this were her quest, not mine! I sighed. What had happened to my resolve? It was as if the moment I'd landed, every feeling I had was bad.

"Wait up!" I hollered to Kerka; I could barely see her now. I felt myself growing furious. She was showing off, thinking that she was stronger and more determined than I was!

"Wait, Kerka!" I yelled. I started running, until I finally caught up with her and was slightly out of breath. "Why didn't you stop?" I asked.

Kerka didn't answer, just kept marching. Why was she being a jerk, not paying any attention to me?

"What's the matter with you?" I asked irritably.

"We must prepare for action," she said, her eyes focused straight ahead, her back stiff as my calla lily mother's.

"It's awful here," I said. "Can't you feel it? There's nothing growing at all. Nothing!" Kerka was silent. "It's worse than the Concrete City," I went on. "And my butt still hurts from that landing."

Kerka stopped short, and without even turning around, she said fiercely, "Will you stop *whining*, Birdie!"

"I am *not* whining!" I said. "This is the ugliest place I've ever seen in my life. I don't know what I'm doing here. We're supposed to be in a dream, not a nightmare!" *There,* I thought. *That should shut her up.*

Kerka turned back, her blue eyes looking calmly and directly into my green ones. "You are Birdie Cramer Bright, future fairy godmother. You are the last hope of the Arbor Lineage. You have a mission. You need to fulfill it."

I turned away, seething. If she thought she was helping, she wasn't. How dared she tell me who I was? She'd known me for . . . what? A day? Two at the most?

"You want to go running back to the fairies? You want to go back to your perfect Califa? Nothing's stopping you," she said, her tone cold as ice. "You have free will. You can quit anytime you want. Just wake yourself up and go back to your sad real life."

"Well, maybe I *will* quit!" I spit. "Maybe I'm just too sensitive to my environment to put up with this . . . this . . . graveyard! And you!"

"Fine," Kerka shot back. "That lets me off the hook."

"Maybe *you* shouldn't have come along," I muttered. I stomped my foot, and dust flew.

"Maybe you're right!" snarled Kerka. "And maybe you should grow up!"

I was battling with myself about just how offended I should feel when I saw that Kerka's eyes were filled with angry tears. When she saw me notice them, she lowered her head and dashed them away with her hand.

Seeing Kerka like that helped me let go of my

own anger. As it drained away, I couldn't imagine where it had all come from. "Sorry for being a jerk," I said quietly.

"I'm sorry, too," she said. "I'm sorry I didn't answer when you called. I was just nervous and needed to keep moving."

"I don't know what came over me, either," I said. "And I guess I *am* used to complaining. It was good for you to stop me. I clearly need you on this adventure."

"You weren't that bad," Kerka said. "It obviously really upsets you when there's nothing growing around you. And that makes sense with your family."

"Friends?" I asked, putting my hand out and smiling.

We shook.

"Do we need some food?" she asked.

"That's a great idea," I said. "And it'll remind us of the fairies."

Kerka put her Kalis stick on the rocky ground. Then she shook her backpack off her shoulders and pulled out the box lunch the fairies had packed. The box was painted with lilacs that had silver and gold leaves. It made me calm and happy. We sat in our beautiful fairy clothes on the dusty trail, unwrapping delicacies.

There were cucumber toast-point sandwiches, rosemary biscuits, and rose-cut radishes. There were grapes and herbed cheeses. There were gooseberry nectar and spiced mango chutney for dipping. For dessert, the fairies had packed lemon zest tarts. It was the best picnic I'd ever had, in the worst surroundings.

"I know we have to go to the jungle to get to the Shadow Tree, but do you think there's a better way?" asked Kerka, licking the last of the lemon tart from her fingertips.

"The map!" I said as I popped the last rose-cut radish into my mouth.

Kerka got out Zally's map and threw the fairy wrappings into her pack. I reached over to help unroll the map on the rocky ground. The map went through its ritual of showing us Zally (she waved at us this time, which was heartening) then it filled itself in. Zally is like a *Dodecatheon*, the shooting-star flower.

"It looks like Mo's garden! But I wonder where we are on the map," I said, remembering that we were drawn in last time. Maybe Zally couldn't do that here in the shadows.

I could make out the maze with the tree in the middle, then the path to the waterfall past the valley, all surrounded by a jungly mass, which, thankfully, didn't look like it was that big. It made sense that in this world the Shadow Tree would have started in a garden like Mo's. Maybe Mo even created or tended it before the Singing Stone was broken!

Just then, a shower of red sparks silently emerged.

Kerka and I drew back, waiting to see what happened. Then words—or letters—formed:

HO WHAT PEAT SH GA

9

The Shadow Land

Kerka and I exchanged a puzzled look.

"Is it a foreign language?" I asked.

"No idea," said Kerka. "It looks like it might be written upside down or backward." She bent over to try to read it upside down.

We stared hard at the letters, trying to make sense of them. As we did, I started to get that unsettling irritated feeling again. I could tell that something mean was going to come out of my mouth any second, and I couldn't stop it.

"*You're* the one who brought the map," I told Kerka. "Why can't you read it?"

She looked shocked at my outburst (and no wonder—I'm embarrassed just thinking about it!).

"Well, I sure don't know what this stupid map is

saying," I continued. "You're supposed to be helping *me*, not the other way around!"

Kerka turned cold and silent.

Now *everything* about her bothered me. Her seriousness was boring. Her strength was hard and unfeeling. I looked back down at the map letters, and now they moved around, as if we were upsetting them.

GO WHET PATS AH HA

"Go wet your pants?" I said through my irritation.

"Maybe it's jumbled?" Kerka suggested, gritting her teeth.

"GO WEST!" I yelled then. "The message says GO WEST PATH, AH HA!" I was proud of myself.

"Ah ha?" said Kerka. "That doesn't make sense."

"Sure it does. It's what you say when you've figured something out, which I did." I looked around. "So which way is west?"

Without a word, Kerka pointed with her stick. I didn't ask how she knew. I just stared where she'd pointed, into the tangled sea of brush and twisted vines and seemingly impassable growth. No question, our only choice was to proceed through the strange jungle in as westward a direction as we could.

We walked in silence. The air was getting colder with each step. Kerka used her Kalis stick as a machete, hacking through the dead, tangled vegetation. I wondered why Zally's map hadn't shown us a picture of something this time; it seemed to do slightly different things each time we used it. I didn't say anything to Kerka, though, not with the mood she was in.

We kept going until we hit a sheer drop-off. Kerka and I looked down wordlessly into a ravine filled with more dead trees and bushes. We'd have to walk along the ravine in one direction or the other. If we'd been walking west, which way would it be? Both ways looked the same: dark, with uninviting plants and scrubby trees everywhere. I felt all turned around. Where was this in Mo's garden?

Then something clicked. "Ah ha!" I said. "We're coming in backward, past the waterfall—although I doubt there's a waterfall here—and the ravine, the ha-ha!" I knew exactly which way to go now! I remembered that at Granny Mo's, the right-hand path at the cliff went to the waterfall with the stone seat, and the left-hand one went to where Willowby had turned to the maze and the Glimmer Tree.

Kerka was looking at me doubtfully. "The map didn't say AH HA. It said HA HA," I explained. My excitement left no room for the itchy irritation at Kerka. "This is the way." I pointed to the left, along the edge of the chasm. "There will be a bridge. Really!"

Kerka just stared blankly at me. "I don't know what ha-ha means, and you sound crazy," she said. "Why should I trust you?"

"Mo says that a ha-ha is what the Irish make to keep sheep out of their gardens. It's like a ditch or a dip in the earth. So with a bit of shadow thrown in, the ha-ha could turn into this ravine, don't you think?"

Kerka was still not with me, and I couldn't really blame her. I sighed. "I don't know what came over me back there," I said. "Look, I'm really sorry about arguing. Really. Really, *really*. Please, forgive me, Kerka?"

Kerka's blue eyes were guarded, and I could tell that she was not sure if she was ready to make up yet. "Do you get the feeling here that sometimes something not good is creeping into you?" I asked. "That's what I keep feeling. The way the shadow has turned the Aventurine version of Mo's garden into this . . . plant graveyard, the shadow is creeping into me, too, and making me, I don't know, like a mean version of myself."

Kerka was nodding as I spoke, and I watched her eyes clear. "I know exactly what you mean," she said. "It's making me want to fight with you. I keep thinking how different we are and how I have to do all the work. But I *know* that teamwork almost always makes things better — not to sound like a coach, but it's true."

I had a sudden thought. "Hey, I bet whatever bad thing is creeping into our heads scrambled Zally's map, too!"

"That makes sense," Kerka agreed.

"So what do we do?" I asked.

"Be on our guard," she answered.

Then I had an idea. "What if we had a signal? You know, something that will tell you I'm starting to get the weird feeling and I need your help," I suggested. "And it would work the other way around, too, if you're getting . . . well, snappish."

"Yeah, that sounds good," said Kerka. "Like a handshake or a peace sign?"

"How about a sign that reminds us of the fairies?" I suggested, remembering the heart gift from the fairy queen. I put my hand on my heart. It felt goofy, but I also felt warmth welling up from my heart and actually giving me strength. "How about if *this* is our signal?"

"I like it," she said, slapping her hand on her own heart vigorously. "It's perfect."

"Perfect," I agreed. We sat there for a minute with our hands on our hearts.

We then continued on, and Kerka let me lead. Soon we could see the broken bridge up ahead that would finally take us across the canyon. "It's the bridge I told you about!" I said. Despite the grim surroundings, I was thrilled that I had been right. Not in an "I told you so" way, but in an "I'm so glad I can trust my instincts" way.

"Good," said Kerka. "I'm glad you were right. Do we cross the bridge?"

"Yes," I said, sobering instantly.

It was nothing at all like Mo's beautiful Ha-Ha Valley. But the vantage point was identical. My eyes fixed on a huge tree in the distance—the Shadow Tree. It was in the middle of a maze of boxwoods, their branches tangled and ghostly gray. Lightning flashed over the tree, and the blackest clouds I've ever seen hung over it. The wind whistled around us, and I shivered.

I walked to the bridge, the wind tearing at my fairy cloak. When we reached the bridge, Kerka

marched over it in her usual way. She didn't even
hold the rotting handrail or miss a step as she avoided
the broken slats.

I, on the other hand, stopped dead. How was I
going to cross this bridge? I could barely cross the
nice bridge in Mo's garden!

I bet you're wondering what the big deal was.
Well, let me tell you: Not only was the bridge rotting
and missing slats, but it was also literally covered
with bugs—termites, spiders, ants, and bugs I didn't
know the names of and didn't *want* to know the
names of.

Kerka reached the other side of the bridge and
turned back, brushing off what must have been some
bugs that had gotten on her. "Come on, Birdie!" she
called. "It's just bugs."

"*Just* bugs? Are you crazy? What about how
high up it is?" I called to her. My stomach quivered
at the thought of having to step on the insects or
touch them. I shook my head. "No. This is too much."

Kerka put her hands on her hips. "More than the
shadow creeping into your head? Bugs are worse?"

I took a deep breath and stepped onto the
bridge. The bugs crunched under my feet. I gagged
and put my hand out to the railing, where, of course,
more bugs were waiting. The bridge creaked under

my feet, and I jumped back, shrieking and shaking off bugs. "I can't do it!" I yelled. The only good thing about the bugs was that they seemed to stay on the bridge.

Kerka shook her head and tromped back over the bridge to me. How did she do it? Was she made of iron? She brushed stray beetles off her arms and legs as if they were dirt. I watched her with my mouth open.

"You just want to live in a sweet little garden where everything is safe and comfortable," said Kerka.

"I'm just scared—" I tried to explain, tears filling my eyes.

"You're scared of change," said Kerka, cutting me off. "Well, change happens, Birdie."

What was she talking about? *I won't let Kerka treat me this way,* I thought. "Maybe you never had to move from a place you love to a place you hate," I shot back. "Just because your mother found a job she liked better!"

"Change happens. Life happens." Kerka stared at me. "Death happens. . . ."

That hit me like a ton of bricks. Kerka's mother had died, and here I was complaining about moving across the country, still complaining about my own mom. I was mortified. I took a deep breath. Then, all of a sudden, I recognized that this was the power of the shadow at work. I moved my hand to my heart and was filled with warmth again.

"You're right, Kerka," I said quietly. "I'm sorry. I'm just scared."

I could see Kerka struggling with something, and then she put her hand on her heart, too. I saw her body relax, and she closed her eyes.

She opened her eyes after a few moments. "Let me help you," she said. "Just imagine that the bugs are fake, plastic toy bugs. I bet you are good at imagining things."

"Okay," I said. That sounded like it might be possible. "I can do that."

"Take my hand, and we'll just go," said Kerka. "Don't think too hard about it. And be careful. Remember how scared I was to go swimming, and it all turned out okay? This will, too, I promise."

She held out her hand, and I took it, trusting her as I had trusted Mo the first time I crossed her bridge. Kerka pulled me onto the bridge, just like that. I marched behind her, eyes on the slats, thinking, *plastic bugs, plastic bugs,* and when I felt a few crawl on me, I thought, *wind-up plastic bugs, wind-up plastic bugs.*

We reached the other side, and Kerka stood back as I screeched my head off and shook bugs every which way. When they were all off me and I stood quivering, I saw that Kerka was laughing.

"Oh, Birdie, I am sorry," she said. "But you are so funny! All that jumping and screaming!"

I laughed weakly, seeing her point. "I swear, I am not usually such a scaredy-cat," I said, shivering from the cold now. "But I really hate bugs—and heights."

"So do a lot of people," said Kerka. "One of my sisters doesn't like heights, and my mother hated bugs, too."

"I like worms," I said, trying to redeem myself a little. "And bees and butterflies are nice."

"Well, then you must be okay," Kerka said, grinning. "Shall we continue now?"

I nodded. We turned toward the maze and the dark tree that loomed at its center. The wind blew leaves in little whirlwinds down a path that wound through the thorny bushes and vines, right to the entrance of the maze.

Lightning cracked over the tree, and thunder rumbled. But there was no rain, no soothing, healing rain.

I pulled my cloak around me. Kerka held out

her Kalis stick like a tennis racket (I guess she was going to whack away anything she saw). We stepped onto the path. Nothing moved except the wind, so we kept going. Kerka let me lead, so I saw the lights first, just as we reached the maze.

The maze walls were ten feet tall here in Aventurine, and the lights came through them, moving like the stars had outside of my bedroom window. I stopped, and Kerka bumped into me. "What are they?" I whispered.

Kerka looked up and saw them.

"They must somehow be the Shadow Tree's helpers," whispered Kerka, sounding as scared as I felt.

"Kerka, we have to run as fast as we can," I said. I knew if the lights saw us, they'd attack us. I don't know how I knew, but I did. "I think I can find the way through the maze."

"I'll be right behind you," Kerka whispered.

I ran, choosing my way by pure instinct. I forced myself not to question but just to feel. Finally, I knew we were close to the middle. I went from running to trotting, then walking, until I stopped. Kerka stopped, too.

I thought we needed to rest before we actually tried to do what we needed to do next. What that was exactly, I didn't know. From where we were, we had a clear view of the tree; the lights rested on the tips of the tree's barren branches. They seemed to be waiting for something. The dark clouds hovered like smoke over the tree.

"It knows we're here," whispered Kerka. "The Shadow Tree knows we are here."

"How do you—" I began.

Suddenly the lights flew from the tree like a swarm of bees. They dove for us.

"Put your back against mine!" Kerka said. "Use your cloak!"

I had a second to pull my cloak off before they were on us. Kerka and I stood back to back; she slashed at them with her Kalis stick, and I flung my cloak at them like a matador.

Whenever a light managed to land on me, it stung. The sting was strange, sending a stabbing, empty feeling into my heart. I was filled with pinpricks of sadness and fear and rage that echoed all the bad feelings I'd had in my life. I couldn't tell if Kerka got stung the same way, because I couldn't see her face, but it was probably the same for her. Maybe it was worse, because she had lost more than I had.

The small but powerful jabs came over and over. Kerka and I were being pushed through the maze by the lights—into the center of the maze.

Then the Shadow Tree was looming over us. As one, the stinging lights silently flew back to the tree's branches, as if their job was done.

"Are you okay?" I asked Kerka, turning to face her.

"I guess so. Just sad," she said, not looking at me but tugging at her braids that had loosened and fallen down her back. "I don't know how you are going to fight the shadow, Birdie."

Now that we weren't being attacked, I looked up at the tree. It was even more menacing up close, despite being so near to death. It was dark in the center of the maze, the stinging lights and lightning giving the only illumination. Between these two light sources, one dim and constant, the other bright and occasional, I could make out several things. One was a large knothole on one side of the tree, seeping black lava. The other was a bank of lush ferns that was growing among the tree's huge knotty roots.

The ferns had to be the last thriving things left in this dead realm of Aventurine. They were welcoming, and so green—the only real life I had felt in a long time.

I smiled. "Kerka," I said. "Do you see those? Maybe there's a chance—"

"Watch out!" Kerka cried, her Kalis stick flying out and nearly crashing into my skull. Instead, it met a bunch of fern fronds that seemed to have sprung away from the others. There was an intense scraping sound as stick met fern. Kerka and I both flung ourselves backward as the ferns reached for us.

Kerka held up her Kalis stick; in a flash of lightning, I saw a deep cut in the stick.

"Those ferns are sharp as knives," Kerka said. Her gaze was focused on the ferns, her eyes narrowed.

I wanted to scream—how could the only live plants here be so vicious? Kerka and I backed up a little more. The stinging lights flew down, blocking the way out of the maze.

Just then came a rustling sound. Something was slithering on the ground, snaking toward us. It was hard to tell in the semidarkness which direction it was approaching from. Kerka took her battle stance, and I followed her lead, clueless as to what was coming.

We looked down finally; the rustling, slithering sounds came from spidery roots and thorny vines that were crawling from beneath the ferns. Kerka swung her Kalis stick, and bits of roots and vine flew. But Kerka didn't stop there; she jumped into the air and came down hacking at the creepers with her Kalis stick.

Now the lights dove at us again, and I stood there, trying to hold them off with my cloak, which was getting more and more tattered. Kerka and I were completely under siege. The vines twisted and writhed, grabbing at our boots while the ferns waited to slash at us whenever we drew too close. Kerka was like a fighting acrobat, leaping and somersaulting, her braids flying. If I hadn't been so terrified, I would have just watched her.

The roots finally got Kerka's ankles and pulled her toward the ferns. I tried to tug her back, but she just shrugged me off. "Keep at the lights, Birdie," she said through gritted teeth. "And think, think of what you can do."

Kerka fought off the ferns with jabs and spiral swings of her Kalis stick while I scrambled desperately to find some other weapon. Then Kerka fell or was pulled over by the vines. The blades of the ferns rang *shing-shing* like metal as they swiftly slashed her boots, her tunic, and her will. The roots were wrapping themselves around Kerka's arms and body, holding her down.

I raced to help, not sure what I could do. Instantly, a frond sprang out, not at me but at Kerka's weapon. The razor fern, in one fell swoop, sliced the Kalis stick in half.

The single fern blade turned toward me. It raised its head and waved slowly from side to side like a blind cobra about to strike. But then it seemed to change its mind, and it stretched itself high above Kerka's head. The lights hovered above us, their eerie light throwing shadows everywhere.

"No!" I shouted.

Kerka screamed, and I lunged toward her, but the vines had wound around my feet, holding them tight to the ground. I fell sprawling, screaming, but my hand was within reach of the half of the Kalis stick that had flown my way. If I could push the end close enough for Kerka to grasp, I could pull her out of there.

"Grab the stick, Kerka!" I yelled, reaching the half Kalis stick as far as I could.

A drip of blood trickled down her face as she gaped at me. She reached out, but the vines pulled her away. The fern blade waved in victory above her head. I suddenly remembered my cloak in my other hand. I tossed it to her like a net.

"Get it!" I shouted.

Even as I yelled, the fern blade dropped.

I shut my eyes, and the next instant I heard

Kerka scream in what sounded like pure fury. "My hair!" she shrieked. "How dare you!"

She was alive!

I opened my eyes to see that the fern blade had indeed hacked off Kerka's braids, right to the nape of her neck. But I saw her only for one moment before the vines and roots pulled her kicking and screaming under the ferns.

Then suddenly there was complete and utter silence.

10

"The Green Song"

The ferns swayed innocently. The lights hovered for a moment, then flew to perch in the dead tree branches again.

"Kerka, are you there?" I shouted.

"Birdie." I thought I heard Kerka's voice coming faintly from inside the tree.

"Kerkaaaaaaa!" I screamed into the darkness.

No reply. She was gone. On the ground, strands of blond hair were scattered, along with scraps of cloth from my once-lovely green velvet cloak.

I was alone, only a stone's throw from the Shadow Tree. What was I going to do? Half the Kalis stick lay by my feet. Half of the Singing Stone was in my pocket. Kerka, my other half on this adventure, was trapped inside the tree.

I suddenly thought of my mother. No wonder

she gave up. No one normal person could possibly have the power to fight off such enemies!

I put my hand to my heart, desperate for courage. I remembered Kerka's words: *Think, think of what you can do.* But I was too tired to think. I sighed, and decided to see if the Shadow Tree itself would offer any clues.

My heart beat loudly as I stepped up to the tree. I didn't care about the ferns, and as if because I didn't care, they didn't sense me. I walked all around the tree and came back to the oozing knothole.

Now the inky ooze didn't just bleed from the knothole but flowed from the bark, forming a hot black pool around the base of the trunk. I know it was hot, because I slipped in it. When I stood up, I was covered in goo and dirt and bits of leaves and hacked-off vines.

It was horrible.

How did I end up here? I wondered. This was supposed to be a nice little trip to meet my granny Mo, and it had turned into a quest to save my family. And now to save Kerka as well!

I looked at my hands, caked with muck, and didn't recognize them. *Who are you, Birdie Cramer Bright? Aren't you that shy girl, carrying Belle on the train? How did this happen?* I had thought *New York* was a hard, cold place. Kerka was right—what a whiner I'd been! I had my dad and my new school waiting for me. There was my mom, who loved me even if she didn't understand me.

Heat seemed to pour off the tree. I was sweating. My hand went to wipe my forehead and stopped at my heart. I closed my eyes. Now the heart light gave me coolness, and new thoughts rose up.

I was Kerka's only hope. I was the only hope of the Arbor Lineage. And I was the only hope to mend the rift between my grandmother and my mother and myself. *The only hope.*

I opened my eyes. The knothole had grown, and as I watched, it grew even more until it was an arched doorway with a small door—an actual wooden door! The door grew and deepened in color. It was now a robin's egg blue—the exact color of the front door to my old house in Califa.

A rusty key protruding from the keyhole turned on its own, and the door swung open. Inside was pure darkness. The ferns parted so that I could step through.

But I didn't want to go inside. It was like with the bugs on the bridge—I couldn't make myself. How would I do this without Kerka?

Behind me came the sound of wings, growing

louder and louder. When I turned, I was staring into a pair of ancient eyes. The eyes were in the small face of an old woman, and the face was on the head and body of a giant gray-black crow. The crow woman put her head back and howled like a wolf.

All I could do was stare in horror, but then my brain registered it. The crow woman was a banshee! My mother had told me the Irish legend of this ghost woman when I first started loving fairy tales. The banshee was sometimes a crow, I remembered, and sometimes a ghostly hag—in this case, she was both. But no matter what shape she took, if the banshee wailed, it meant one thing: Someone was about to die.

"Death began when the stone was broken!" the banshee wailed. "It was I, the crow, who found it and brought it here to the tree! Then all became death, death, death!"

As the banshee's gray-black wings began to beat at me, I wondered if I was the one about to die. But I couldn't let it happen—I just couldn't!

I had nowhere to run but into the Shadow Tree, so that is what I did, right into its inky blackness. The door slammed shut behind me. I could still hear the screeching howls of the banshee on the other side.

Suddenly in the darkness I saw that a light was growing. I had put my hand on my heart, truly by accident, and now I was emitting a golden green light. It was crazy to see my skin glowing and lighting up the dark inside of the tree. I put my hand in my pocket to check if my half of the Singing Stone was still there.

When my finger touched it, I realized something amazing, and I wondered how I hadn't seen it before. Maybe being in the tree is what helped me, or maybe it was the Singing Stone. In any case, what I realized was that the tree was not evil; it was in pain! It needed healing, and who better to do that than someone from the Arbor Lineage, a fairy-godmother-in-training with green magic—in other words, me!

The fairy queen had given me Mo's entry in *The Book of Dreams*, something to remember, she had said. Mo's entry was "The Green Song," so I decided to sing it to the tree itself. I just made up a melody, but it all fit together seamlessly, like magic.

As I sang, my own glow filled the space even more. I could see a spiral staircase leading up. I sang, holding the half of the Singing Stone in my hand, and climbed the stairs (which were disgustingly covered in the black ooze).

Gradually, I felt the tree relax. Then, all of a sudden, the tree let out a long sigh; it was like a child finally falling asleep. I sang "The Green Song" very softly, and listened. I swear I could hear the Shadow Tree's breathing, deep and low.

I kept singing as I climbed up, up, up. At the top of the stairs were passages that twisted left and right, up and down. It was all much larger than it had seemed on the outside.

"Kerka?" I sang her name among the other words of the song.

"Birdie? Is that you?" I heard Kerka's voice faintly calling from the right-hand passage.

"Kerka!" I sang. "I'm coming! Kerka, keep calling! Don't stop!"

Kerka called, and I sang more softly so I could hear her. I walked along the passage. The tree walls didn't seem so black now, but more like a rich green. Just as I noticed that, though, I came to a low, arched door, from which Kerka's voice was coming.

I ducked under the arch and through the door into a small dark room, which my glow instantly lit. It was filled with sticks and shiny blackbird feathers—a giant bird's nest. And there, tangled in the sticks, was Kerka.

"Birdie, help me get out of here!" said Kerka, her hair in spiky tufts around her face.

I nodded, and kept singing, as I climbed into the nest. The sticks poked at me, but I was now so covered with scratches and scrapes I hardly noticed. I put the stone half in my pocket so I could pull at the sticks that were holding Kerka. While I yanked away at them, I motioned for Kerka to sing with me.

At first she shook her head (maybe she didn't think her voice was good—as if the tree cared!), but then she sang, at first softly, and then loudly and strongly as I knew she could. The sticks turned into dust as I pulled at them, so I got her out pretty quickly.

We both climbed out of the nest, and then Kerka hugged me. It felt silly singing and hugging, but there was no way I was stopping! I was about to walk out through the archway, figuring that we'd just walk all around inside the tree, singing, when Kerka stopped me. I turned to face her, and she held out her hand.

"I found this in the nest," she sang, and unfurled her fingers like they were a flower blooming.

In her palm rested the other half of the Singing Stone.

I took my half of the stone out of my pocket. We held up the two halves and pressed them together, singing "The Green Song." The crack sealed, and the stone glowed much brighter than I did.

Kerka let go of her half of the stone, and I held

a complete Singing Stone. We had both stopped singing and were just staring at the Singing Stone.

Then I noticed that the *tree* was glowing now, all on its own, bright and green.

"Play the Singing Stone," Kerka said.

I put my lips to the etching and blew. The most incredible sound came out—as if the stone were a harp, a flute, and a violin all at the same time. Now the Singing Stone's music played "The Green Song," and things started to happen very quickly.

The tree walls were closing in, fresh healthy wood filling in the spaces.

"Come on!" Kerka said. I nearly stopped playing the Singing Stone to laugh—Kerka was back, and as sure of herself as ever!

We quickly ducked under the arch, and the room disappeared behind us. I guess I could have stopped playing the Singing Stone and the tree might have stopped healing so quickly, but it didn't seem fair to make the tree wait. Kerka and I ran down the staircase as fast as we could. No longer was there black ooze on the stairs, just clean, green wood.

We ran out the door just in time, for the tree filled up right behind us. Kerka and I both sat on the ground to catch our breath. I stopped playing the

Singing Stone for a moment. The hum of "The Green Song" continued through everything, so I just held the stone in my hand and watched this new world with wonder.

The air was clear and clean, and the most refreshing rain ever was sprinkling down, washing away the dust and dirt and ooze. The sky was the bright gray of rain clouds backlit by sunshine. All around us, plants were sprouting up and turning green. The knife-ferns had disappeared, replaced by riotous daisies that pushed out of the ground and bloomed as we watched. Overhead, in the tree, buds appeared and leaves opened up.

I saw that Kerka's hair had grown back—it was braided and coiled back on her head perfectly. I looked down at myself and saw that I was, thankfully, being washed clean as well. I saw Kerka's Kalis stick, whole again, lying on the ground.

Suddenly I heard the sound of wings, and the banshee landed in front of us. Before Kerka or I had time to react, its old woman's face changed until it was a crow's head and face. The seemingly normal crow (although I'm sure it wasn't *completely* normal) looked into my eyes. Her eyes were no longer haunted, but warm and bright as a mischievous bird's. Then the banshee-now-crow soared into the gentle rain, flying away until she was just a black speck in the sky.

"What was that?" asked Kerka.

I grinned, braces and all. "Just a banshee," I said. "Nothing I can't handle." I stood up and put the whole Singing Stone into my pocket. Then I held out my hand to Kerka. "It's New Year's Eve — let's go home."

Kerka held her hand out, and I hauled her up. We were both soaking wet but relatively clean, and only a little worse for wear. Kerka picked up her Kalis stick and put it in her backpack, which was still on her back.

I hit my forehead with the palm of my hand. "Oh geez," I said. "How do we get home? Do we have to go back the same way?"

And then I heard bells ringing, and the rain stopped. I heard the sound of wings and looked up, thinking the crow might be back. Instead, I saw fairies, lots of them, Queen Patchouli in the lead. They were flying down to us, their gossamer wings glimmering. Queen Patchouli stepped lightly onto the ground. Her wings folded and she hugged us both for a long, long time.

Then Queen P. shook the bells on her wrist, and my suitcase appeared right in front of us. With a snap and a clatter, it unclasped and flew open. A smile spread over my face. I couldn't hold it back, even though it showed my full set of braces, which I was sure were glowing in the sunlight. I didn't care.

This time the suitcase didn't turn into a wardrobe. It simply stayed what it was, and Patchouli reached inside and pulled out a small envelope. She handed the envelope to me as the rest of the fairies danced around us.

I opened the envelope and took out a small piece of paper that was pressed with flowers. I unfolded the paper. "To Birdie," I read aloud. "We thank you for healing the Arbor Lineage, for retrieving the Singing Stone, our talisman, and for restoring harmony to the green worlds."

"*Our* talisman?" I asked. I folded the letter, and it turned into a daisy in my hand.

"Exactly," Patchouli answered. "This message is not from the fairies. It is from the women in your family, for they are your fairy godmothers in the real world, there to help you learn and grow. There to watch over you and keep you as safe as they can."

"Thank you," I whispered to the daisy.

Queen P. then turned to Kerka. "The next time you visit Aventurine, it will be for your own quest, your own discovery," she said. "Though I trust that you have learned things with Birdie."

"I have," said Kerka. She looked over at me. "And I wouldn't have missed it for the world," she added. "Not one minute of it!"

"Not even the arguing?" I teased.

"Well . . . actually . . . let's not go there, okay?" she said, chuckling.

"It is time for you to return home now," said Queen Patchouli.

"Okay," I said, "but can I just have a moment with Kerka before we go?"

The queen nodded and stepped away, joining the other fairies as they danced around the newly blossoming garden.

"So, we both have fairy godmothers," I said to Kerka.

"And are going to be fairy godmothers ourselves one day," said Kerka. "At least, we will if we can survive all the fairy tests."

"Yes. It's like being in a funny kind of school, isn't it?" I said.

"It is," Kerka said. "A school for fairy god-mothers."

"A fairy godmother academy," I said. "Complete with fairy uniforms, which aren't like uniforms at all, of course!"

"I love it! The Fairy Godmother Academy!" said Kerka. "Birdie, do you think we can meet up here again?"

"I don't know!" I said. "But I promise to try!"

We suddenly heard the tinkling of bells all around us. Flower petals drifted in the air like snow, and . . .

Part Three

Roots and Flowers

11

The New Year

. . . suddenly I was shaking, my jaw frozen shut, my whole body trembling with cold. My eyes shot open. I was sitting on Mo's stone seat, my gloves beside me. My feet were frozen to the ground, so I must have been there for quite a while. An hour? Five hours? I had no idea. Had I fallen asleep?

I freed my frozen feet, jumped up, and looked around. The waterfall bared its frozen fangs, and the evergreens were frosted white. The sky was gray. It looked like a nice New Year's Eve snow was on the way.

I shivered. My braces were positively freezing. I clenched my hands in the cold and remembered everything as my right fist closed on the Singing Stone. I opened my hand and looked at it.

It was the whole stone, healed, with every tiny

etched detail in place—every branch of the tree and the walled maze perfectly drawn, not a line missing! I did a little dance of joy, right there, and nearly slid down the hill.

"The Singing Stone!" I shouted to the frozen waterfall, to the trees, to the boulders, to the snow-laden clouds. I tucked the stone deep into the pocket of my jeans and gave a quick glance around, just in case there was a shimmering tail or a girl with an orange stick hiding someplace in the frosty area. A winter sparrow darted out of a tree, startling me for a moment. Then I smiled as it flew off into the sky.

I thought of shimmying down the ice-glazed boulders, but instead, I ran, jumping from boulder to boulder. I had to get to the Glimmer Tree! I felt like a gazelle, leaping in a graceful streak toward the evergreens. Well, not quite a gazelle, I realized, laughing out loud when I slipped and slid on my bottom, *ba-BUM*, down three boulders (ouch!) and landed at the snowy base of an evergreen.

I planted a big kiss on the evergreen's trunk.

Then I was up, brushing snow off my seat, and running again. I raced through the willows, along the ravine, and tromped like Mo right across the bridge. I rounded each corner and switchback of the maze, excited, leaping over icy patches on the ground.

There she stood, at the center, in all her golden brown majesty.

"*Ms. Quercus! Quercus Robur!*" I whispered. I held up the Singing Stone to show her. (You never know what the Glimmer Tree might be able to see or sense!) I'm pretty sure that I heard a soft sigh of relief coming from deep within the tree.

I reached my arms around her trunk, hugging her tight. I was so grateful for the Glimmer Tree, so grateful for my frightening and magical and wonderful trip to Aventurine. So amazed that I—plain old Birdie Bright—was going to be a fairy godmother, and that I was from a whole line of fairy godmothers!

I walked to the side of the tree that was rotting and felt for the soft spot. I felt up and down and around and around where it had been. It was gone, all of it. The Glimmer Tree was healed!

I closed my eyes as I laid my cheek against the tree's beautiful, rugged bark where the rotting part had been. I felt tears begin to rise in me, from my heart up through my veins, and I wasn't sure why. Just then, a blob of snow fell on my nose.

I looked up into the tree. "Willowby!" I exclaimed.

"Mrrrrow," said Willowby in a friendly way. He

crouched as if he were going to
jump, and I held out my arms,
wondering if I could catch him.
Then he seemed to change his
mind (I must have looked
worried) and shimmied down
the trunk instead. On the
ground, he purred at me
and wound about my legs
the way cats do when they feel like they own you.

"Thank you, Willowby," I said in a proper voice.
"Come on, let's go home now."

I stopped all along the way, checking out the
plants. I swear I could see spring beneath the winter
snow! Where Mo had pointed out summer squash
and Fourth of July cucumbers, I saw them in my
mind and couldn't wait to come back in the summer
when they'd really be there. We passed the Christmas roses (*Helleborus niger*), and I thought of the girl
whose tears had made white flowers sprout. There
were the rose hips that looked like orange and red
Christmas ornaments against the deep evergreen.

How lucky that I could have all of this whenever I visited! Mo was so close now, just a train ride
away. Suddenly I realized this was even better than
Califa! I had Mo's garden and my own garden of

Aventurine now. Plus, I had Mo!

As we got to the back porch, I stopped and made a U-turn. "Wait a sec," I told Willowby. "Let's go see if Granny Mo is still in the greenhouse."

Willowby had clearly had enough, because he dashed through his cat door on the porch.

Me? I raced back to the Victorian greenhouse.

"Mo! Mo?" I called as I walked through the steamy double doors into the stillness.

She wasn't there, but Belle was, sitting on the table beside the baby tea plants. She looked so beautiful! Granny Mo had transplanted her into a solid terra-cotta pot. My daisy now had two brand-new blooms, just like that, plus four little buds on the way! I picked her up and hummed "The Green Song" to her.

Everything in the greenhouse was blooming like nobody's business, as if spring had come early. Buds opened, tiny and soft baby pink, ready to burst into small hot-pink blossoms with deep-red centers any day now.

"*Phlox paniculata*, the bright-eyed garden phlox," I said out loud.

And suddenly, there in the stillness, I *knew*. I knew something had happened, something magical and real at the same time. And it was because of *me*.

I drifted into Mo's little alcove. There, on the table beside the comfy chair, was a piece of paper. I thought at first that it was a journal page from *The Book of Dreams*. I picked it up. It was a printout of an e-mail.

I know you're not supposed to read other people's letters, but I couldn't help myself. I swear the letter jumped into my hand!

Dear MoMo,

I have been thinking about the terrible argument we had on my fourteenth birthday. I was so mad that I wanted to run away, but instead, I took the thing that I knew you cherished most—the Singing Stone—and that night I dreamed myself to Aventurine.

When I got to the place where the Agminium grow, I threw the Singing Stone at the rocks as hard as I could. It broke into two pieces; one fell between the rocks, and the other fell into the water. The wind died down, clouds gathered over the sun, and the humming sounds of nature stopped as if they'd been turned off.

My remorse was immediate. My shame was complete. At that moment I changed my mind, but all I could do was to save the half of the stone nearest me as I felt myself disappearing from Aventurine.

I felt emptiness, loss, and I wanted to take back what I had done. But it was too late. I could tell that I would not be able to go back again.

I know that in many ways it is too late now. But, MoMo, I want to try and make it better. Not just for me, but for Birdie and you and Michael. I am glad that Birdie is there.

I'm coming home, too.

Love,

Emma

I sat staring at that letter for a long time, reading it over and over. In one way, I was furious, but the more I read my mother's words, the more my anger turned to sadness.

My mother had given up her place in the great Arbor Lineage adventure. She had made her decision. My mother would never be a fairy godmother, would never have the magic that I could feel inside me now.

I slowly got up and went to the table to pick up Belle. I tucked her inside Mo's green coat and made my way slowly through the snowy garden toward Mo's house — where Mo must have been all along.

I stepped inside the kitchen to find Mother and Mo sitting at the kitchen table. I was so surprised that I nearly dropped Belle. They didn't even notice the blast of cold air, because my mom was crying. I couldn't remember ever seeing my mother cry before, and it shook me up.

"What's wrong?" I cried.

"Oh, Birdie!" my mother said. She stood up and wrapped her arms around me. I could feel her sobs even through the green coat.

"Is Dad okay?" I asked into her shoulder—it was the only reason I could think of for her crying.

Mom held me away from her and looked me right in the eye. She shook her head and made a little sniffly-giggly sound. "Everyone's okay," she said. "Everyone's okay. I love you, Birdie, my sweet pea."

Hearing her call me sweet pea made *me* cry—she hadn't called me that since I couldn't even remember!

Mo got up and put her arms around both of us, and we all sniffled away for a little while.

It felt so good.

"Well," said Mo finally, pulling back. "Isn't this grand! Now that Birdie's here, I'll put some more water on to boil."

That gave my mom a chance to pull herself together and me a chance to take off my boots and jacket and find a spot for Belle on the windowsill.

"Go on, Emma," said Mo to my mom. "Finish what you were saying earlier. Then we'll hear what Birdie's been up to." Mo winked at me.

"Do you want to hear this, too, Birdie?" Mom asked.

I nodded vigorously.

"Well, as I was telling MoMo, I don't know when I stopped believing. Believing, well, what we believe in this family," my mom said. "I got so far off my path, working for that company that cuts down so many forests to make paper. I pushed hard for them to initiate a reforestation plan, but I just kept getting the runaround."

"We all make mistakes, sweetie," Mo told her. "That's how we learn, right? Never too late to fix things."

"Hey, Mom?" I asked. "Why aren't you in England?"

"I thought it would be nice for me to spend New Year's Eve here," she said, very softly. "With you and your grandmother. And it *is* nice. I am actually happy. Though I wish your dad were here now. He's probably terrified as to what we're all up to." She laughed and hiccupped. "But he *is* coming, Birdie, on the train tonight."

I stared at her. My mom's auburn hair hung around her forehead and cheeks in perfect wavy tendrils; her earrings were the expensive crystal pair from Prague. But her eyes didn't look so perfect. Traces of mascara were smudged along her bottom lids, and the whites of her eyes were red from crying.

"Wow" was all I could say now.

I looked closer. With my new kind of spring-seeing, I could see that my mom really was happy, like when tears have washed away a lot of sadness.

"So your mom is quitting her job," Mo announced, bringing us all cups of tea.

"Huh?" I said. "What? When?" How could that have happened while I was dreaming?

"Soon," my mom answered. "As soon as I find an environmentally responsible company to work for. I was just telling your grandmother . . . on the ride here, I had a hit of sudden clarity. I had gotten so far removed from who I really am . . . from who *we* really are, we Arbor Lineage women. . . ." She shook her head. "Anyway, I made a lot of mistakes, and things are going to change."

"They already have," said Mo.

We all sat there at the kitchen table, not needing to say a word. It was a warm, comfortable silence. I think we were each trying to comprehend what had happened.

Then Mo, who can never stay still for very long, jumped up from the table and went to fill the red kettle with water. "More tea?" she asked.

"Sure," Mom and I said together.

Mom is another one who needs to be busy. I

noticed she was quietly wiping the tabletop until every spot was gone. Some things never change.

I wanted to tell them about Aventurine. But there was so much to tell. I got up and walked over to the eyeglass window. I peered out through the pink octagon-shaped lenses at the snow. Maybe everything *was* rose-colored, I thought. And maybe I didn't have to share every detail. Maybe even if I'd been on an Arbor family quest, some special magic in the world was just for me.

Instead of talking, I reached into my pocket and pulled out the Singing Stone. I raised it to my lips. Just as I began to play, the teakettle started whistling. But the song of the stone was louder and brighter. It completely drowned out the whistling with its melody even before Mo took the teakettle off the burner.

Mo and Mom turned. Their eyes were huge, and they both had big smiles on their faces.

"I knew it! I knew it!" shouted Mo as she turned off the stove. "Let me see it. Let me see that Singing Stone!" Mo raced over and took the stone into her hands and held it like a baby bird in a nest.

"Oh, Birdie, I'm so proud of you!" my mom said then, coming over to wrap me in her arms. Her embrace felt as warm as Dad's hugs, as comforting as I remembered her hugs being when I was little. Did I actually have two parents now, two real parents? I wanted to just stay there, having my mom hold me, for the longest time.

Mo was still shaking her head in amazement, holding the stone. When she passed it back to me, there were tears in her eyes.

"Come on, let's move in by the fire," she said.

"Better yet," Mom piped up, "can the tea wait a few minutes? Before it gets too dark, let's the three of us go for a walk under the moosewood trees!"

"Grand idea!" Mo exclaimed.

"Grand idea!" I agreed, teasing Mo by mimicking her voice as I said it.

"Oh, and who's so smart now that she's been to Aventurine?" Mo teased back, raising her eyebrows. "We'll never hear the end of how she saved the family talisman!" Then she leaned over and kissed me gently on the cheek. She quickly pulled away to get her coat, because I knew she didn't want me to see the tears in *her* eyes.

We bundled up and headed out the front door. The *acer*s that grew right through the front porch were all decorated with silvery stars.

"We're having a New Year's Eve celebration tonight!" said Mo, walking down the steps between the starry sugar maples. "Thought I'd decorate a bit."

"*What?* A party?" I asked. What exactly *had* happened while I was off dreaming in Aventurine? Then a thought hit me.

"Are we telling Dad about the Singing Stone?" I asked.

Mom, Granny Mo, and I looked at each other.

"No," we all said at once.

Then Mom added, "We can talk about it, though. Maybe there's a way to tell him. Usually the men in the family are left out. Maybe they should know, even if they can't actually be a part of it — fairy godmothers could probably use some understanding support, wouldn't you say, MoMo?"

Mo nodded thoughtfully. "We'll see."

Now we were on the driveway that was lined with the striped maples (*Acer pennsylvanicum*) that looked like majestic sentries. I remembered Mo saying that this had been Emma's "moose walk" when she was little.

"And, of course, Hank is joining us tonight," added Mo. "And I'll be playing a little music."

I smiled but didn't say a word, since we were standing beneath the trees. Mom had started spinning around, her arms outstretched. I started spinning, too. And pretty soon, there were three of us, spinning around like dizzy, magical moose wings.

When Mom and Granny Mo headed back, I decided to stay a few more minutes. I wanted a moment to myself before all the New Year celebrating started. As they were walking away, their voices carried.

"What is life without family?" I heard my mom saying. "And what is life without green magic? About time I figured that out, huh?"

"Aren't you proud?" asked Granny Mo. "Aren't you proud of your Birdie?"

"I am proud," said my mom. "Very, very proud."

I took the Singing Stone from my pocket and stood there, holding it in my hand. The air shimmered as snow began to fall. And for a moment, just a moment, I was sure I saw a flower petal or two falling among those snowflakes, floating and waltzing around me.

Epilogue

On the morning of my first day at the Girls' International School of Manhattan, my mom was waiting for me in the kitchen with a cup of Granny Mo's gumbo-limbo tea and a bowl of cereal. She'd be taking me to school before she went to work at her new job in her new Manhattan office. She looked perfect, going off to help save threatened forest ecosystems. She'd still be traveling now and then, but I could tell it would feel different. Her sense of purpose matched her job, she told me, and it showed.

I had lately decided she was a *Potentilla reptans*, a creeping cinquefoil. Mo told me the Irish name for it is Cúig Mhéar Mhuire. It has beautiful yellow flowers and can grow practically anywhere — roadsides, wasteland — beautiful and strong as steel.

My school uniform was a fashion failure

compared to my mom's elegant suit or the fairy clothes of my first trip to Aventurine. Still, it was classic: a navy blue skirt with dark leggings and thick-soled boots. I'd accessorized as best I could with the green peacoat and twelve-foot-long striped scarf that Mo had given me.

Mom and I walked from our apartment through the park across the street to get to my school. I had to admit that the little park had seemed dead and gray when I'd first arrived in New York City. But I had a different viewpoint now. Plus, Dad told me that sometimes in January there would be a quick thaw for a day or two in New York. And guess what? Today was the day. It was still chilly, but a springy chilly, not a wintry chilly. The sky was robin's-egg blue, patches of grass peeked out from the snow, and a few persevering leaves still dangled from the tree branches.

People bustled around us as Mom and I walked silently, playing our old game—the listening game. We tried to hear the wind blow and the birds sing over the sound of cars and voices.

We soon saw a sea of girls in navy blue uniforms, wrapped in coats and scarves and jackets, gathering on steps and around the buses. So we were there. Some of the girls glanced or waved at the boys who were congregating across the street and down two buildings at the Boys' International School.

I was a little nervous, which was weird, considering all I'd been through so recently. But this was the real world, and I was glad when my mom kissed me at the school steps and promised to come pick me up at four o'clock so we could talk about my day over a cup of cocoa.

As I entered the magnificent old marble-floored hallway, I passed a shelf with potted plants, terrariums, dried seedpods, and framed botanical drawings leaning against the wall. A poster hanging above said OUR GREEN EARTH. I stopped to check it out. Right below was a sign-up list for students interested in forming a green squad to help out the local environment. I picked up the pen and wrote my name first on the list.

Then I noticed a gerbera daisy in a pot in the far corner. (TRIBE: *MUTISIEAE*, GENUS: *GERBERA*, read the sign beside it.) It reminded me of Belle, although she was a *simplex*, not a *gerbera*, of course. The daisy was starting to droop, so I reached into my backpack and pulled out my bottled water.

"There you go, little lady," I said as I gave her a nice long drink. Almost instantly, the daisy's thirsty leaves perked up. "You'd probably like to hear a song as well, but I'm new here and don't want to look too strange," I whispered.

I headed to my homeroom, which I could find because of the personal orientation I'd had just a few days earlier. Happily, my homeroom was the class-room of the Latin teacher, Ms. Jones. I hung my green coat and scarf in the cloakroom and then took a seat near the back. I noticed a girl a few rows ahead of me with long blond hair in braids twisted on top of her head. From the back, she looked just like Kerka!

But she couldn't be. Right?

Then the girl turned around, and my jaw just about hit the floor. "Kerka?" I asked.

"Birdie?" she said. I noticed she had an accent here in the real world.

"How—I am so glad you're here!" I exclaimed.

"Me too! It is a wonderful surprise!" Kerka was beaming, as I must have been.

"Welcome to a new semester, a new year," Ms.

Jones announced. "We have two new students who've joined us, and I'd like to start off by asking them to tell us a bit about themselves." She nodded first to Kerka.

As my friend stepped to the front of the room to introduce herself, I felt for the Singing Stone in my pocket. It was smooth all around the edges, and I moved my fingers gently across the etching. I knew the Glimmer Tree branches and every turn of that maze by heart.

I gave Kerka a great big smile. It was going to be a very good year.

Acknowledgments

I could be considered a late bloomer, but I just think of it as one continuous bloom over many years. The long wait to fulfill this dream has allowed time to have the blessing of a very large family, some of whom I birthed and others of whom I inherited or picked up along the way. Thank you to those who call me Gigi—my amazing, creative, and sweet family of children, grandchildren, stepchildren, nieces and nephews, and adopted small souls: Shane, Evan, Dustin, Lucy, Casey, Bella, Kailey, Kirian, Emma, Cameron, Andrea, Noelle, Ben, Julian (the Boo), and Indira. I have learned everything worth knowing by loving and being loved by you.

I would like to thank the following people for helping to shape me on the path of my life: Ray Sr., Dora, Sherry (Sissy Lucha) and Ray Jr. (June Bug),

Aunt Lita and Uncle Louie, my godparents, and Aunt Bet. They handed down stories from our own Welsh and Cuban families and encouraged me to vision and write. There are friends who generously hoped I was on to something—for years and years: Rob Sides, Jana Dezeeuw, Alan Shapiro, LG, Meredith. Thanks to Jesyca Durchin for thinking my songs were good and putting them into everything. Thanks to my mentor, Doug Glen, who convinced me to trust in the conscience of the marketplace.

Hugs to my literary agent, Marcy Posner, who simply "took a chance" on an unknown writer and I think is glad she did. Thanks and blessings to my editor, Mallory Loehr, who was eight months pregnant with her little girl when she saw the value in the idea of the female lineages.

I want to thank my three sons, Shane, Evan, and Dustin, for their creative contributions of music, art, and Web design to the project. To Andrea Burden, who is a fairy queen in real life, I offer my deepest respect for her amazing artwork. I am forever in debt to my man spirit, Robert Skiles, who taught me to sing through a train wreck and write from the soul every day. Thanks to my helper fairies: John Salas (Don Quixote), Lurleen Ladd, and Jan

Wieringa. I offer my most gracious thanks to Linda Lowery Keep, who invited me to journey to San Miguel Allende for guidance and writing.

I am so excited about my new book family at Random House Children's, where a whole company supports the wisdom of wisdom and the beauty of giving voice to the inner life of girls.

And finally, I want to acknowledge all the girls I have met along the way who have read my stories or sung my songs from London to Toronto to Texas. You are the first class of the Fairy Godmother Academy, a very prestigious group of flames who will light up the world in the future. I do this for you. I hope you will share your own stories and songs with your children someday.

About the Author

Jan Bozarth was raised in an international family in Texas in the sixties, the daughter of a Cuban mother and a Welsh father. She danced in a ballet company at eleven, started a dream journal at thirteen, joined a surf club at sixteen, studied flower essences at eighteen, and went on to study music, art, and poetry in college. As a girl, she dreamed of a life that would weave these different interests together. Her dream came true when she grew up and had a big family and a music and writing career. Jan is now a grandmother and writes stories and songs for young people. She often works with her own grown-up children, who are musicians and artists in Austin, Texas. (Sometimes Jan is even the fairy godmother who encourages them to believe in their dreams!) Jan credits her own mother, Dora, with handing down her wisdom: Dream big and never give up.

Turn the page for an excerpt from *Kerka's Book*!
Coming December 2009!

(Dear Reader, please note that the following excerpt
may change for the actual printing of *Kerka's Book*.)

From *Kerka's Book*

The three mountains were still some distance away, and I had to crane my neck to see the peaks. The golden glow over the tops of the Three Queens shone brilliantly even in daylight. With no other clues to consider, instinct and logic told me to head toward the mountains.

A *clickety-click* sound grabbed my attention just as something grabbed my left boot. Startled, I looked down. A six-inch crablike creature had clamped on to my foot with a large claw. The crab's eyes, which were attached to floppy three-inch stalks, stared back at me like those of a small alien. The other claw made a clicking noise as the creature repeatedly opened it and snapped it closed. My boot's leather was thick enough to protect my toes from the crab's pincers, but shaking my foot didn't dislodge the little beast. I didn't want to harm it, but I couldn't continue my journey with a passenger dangling from my boot. I would have thought a creature made of glass would be a little more careful about who it grabbed!

"You've bitten off way more than you can chew, little guy." I shook my finger at the creature as I scolded it. Then I blinked and smiled, inspired by my own words. "But I have something that's much tastier than my boot."

Being careful not to poke the water pods, I opened the food pack, broke off a small piece of what looked like a cake made of sunflower seeds, and carefully placed it on top of my boot. The crab's eyes atop their floppy stalks stopped jiggling as they studied my offering, but the crab didn't let go or try to grab the cake. Anxious to get moving, I tried stamping my heel to jar the creature loose, but the claw clamped down tighter, and it hung on.

The crab's one-claw *clickety-click* taunt became a noisy clatter as more crabs suddenly swarmed to join the chorus. Interestingly enough, not a single one skittered near the rocks.

I was wondering if I would have to just break its little claw off—hoping that it would grow a new one like the stingray—when I tried one last idea. Walking on the heel of my left boot so I wouldn't break the crab, I slowly made my way to a large rock. As soon as I climbed onto it, the crab let go of my boot, dropped into the sand, and scurried back to the crab-creature colony.

From here I was right beside the stone wall. The moss was more of a slime—so although there appeared to be places where I could put a hand or foot, the wall was too slippery to climb. Switching the heavy coat to my other arm, I jumped to the next big rock. I headed down the beach this way, looking for a break in the stone wall. I had to get over it to reach the Three Queens.

Suddenly I remembered the knotted wind rope. I couldn't climb the barrier, but a strong wind could carry me over—as the Redbird Wind had flown Birdie and me across miles of Aventurine. I opened the blue drawstring pouch and pulled out the rope. Just as I was about to touch the first knot, I asked myself: Was it wise to use one of the magic knots so soon?

I put the rope back in its pouch. Then I took a piece of cake from the other pouch and nibbled as I continued jumping from rock to rock. I found cracks between boulders here and there, but they were too narrow for anything except a butterfly flying sideways to squeeze through. Looking up, I realized that the stone wall blocked my view of the Three Queens. On the off-chance that seeing the crowned peaks would give me a brainstorm, I jumped off the rocks.

I braced to jump back on in case any silvery crabs attacked me from the sand. Keeping an eye out, I hurried down the beach, walking away from the rocks until the golden peaks of the three mountains were visible. From here, I could also make out three distinct paths leading away from the piles of rocks: One went straight and the others branched to the left and right. Each path was obviously a route to one of the Three Queens, and each path was blocked by a pair of humungous boulders.

One of the mountains was the key to completing my quest and making my dream come true, but which one? I had no information, no map to help me decide, and not even a friend to talk to about it.

A shrill whistle rang out as pebbles and small rocks tumbled down the boulder barrier.

"Who's there?" I yelled.

Suddenly a small man jumped over the stone wall. Standing two feet tall and wearing what I thought of as basic elf clothing—red cap, brown leggings, a green coat, and black boots—he watched me from atop a large rock. His pointed ears were too long to fit under his cap.

I was sure he was an elf. He looked seriously grumpy, and I tried not to be too worried. In Finnish folklore, disturbing an elf is almost as bad as insulting or cheating one.

The elf's ears twitched when he cocked his head. I just stared back until he somersaulted off his perch. The little man rocked up onto his feet and zipped across the sand, moving so fast I saw only a blur of red and green, like a piece of Christmas gone crazy. He skidded to a halt in front of me.

"Who are you?" I asked.

"Who's who? And who are you?" the elf answered in a squeaky lilt. Then he added with a smirk, "As if I didn't know!"

I wasn't sure whether to tell him my name—which would give the elf the upper hand—or to call his bluff, which might not *be* a bluff.

"Who am I, then?" I asked with an impish grin, and crossed my arms, daring him. I knew that elves have a habit of getting even by doing something ten times worse than what was done to them. But they also like to be amused and entertained—that's what I was shooting for.

The elf jumped up and down and spoke in jumbled rhyme. "The name I choose is Kerka Laine. So I win, you lose, I know your name."

My mouth dropped open, but I quickly closed it. The fairies must have told him to expect me.

"Don't hesitate or you'll be late!" The elf leaned toward me, his brow furrowing. "Your task must be finished, over and done, before the Three Queens' glow disappears in the sun."

He waved his hand.

"By morning?" I asked, perplexed.

"Maybe." The elf shrugged.

I asked a different question, hoping to get a clearer answer. "How long do I have?"

"Tomorrow, today. It's hard to say."

"What does that mean?" I asked as evenly as I could. I couldn't let myself get riled up by this little guy.

The elf threw up his hands. "Sometimes the sun rises, sometimes it blinks on. Or takes the day off, and there isn't a dawn." Then he concluded in an ominous tone: "In Aventurine, anything goes, and no one, but no one, ever knows."

I exhaled slowly. So no one in Aventurine knew when the golden glow on the Three Queens would be lost in sunlight, because the sun didn't always follow the rules. But it didn't matter. I still had to find my little sister's voice before dawn, whenever it happened. I had to have time to finish. Otherwise, my mission would be a fool's errand, and Queen Patchouli was no fool. But now I had to go as fast as possible in case there was exactly enough time and not a minute more, which brought me back to my original problem.

"Thank you," I said to the elf. "That is very helpful information. So can you tell me which path I should take?" I asked as respectfully as I could, trying to get elf points. "You seem to know so many things."

"What trade can you make?" the elf asked.

In stories, elves never do something for nothing, and they are willing to barter for both honor and treats. It was a good thing the Willowood fairies had given me food for the journey. "I have a honey bar." I took a bar from my pouch and held it out.

"Secondhand fairy food? That's rude!" he said with a look of disdain.

"It's perfectly good and very sweet!" I said, a little taken aback.

The elf leaned toward me again. "You can give a fairy's gift away, but not for a bargain on any day."

"Really?" I asked, truly surprised. "I had no idea.

Well, I don't have anything to trade, then. The fairies gave me everything I have, except my backpack."

The elf sniffed. "One more thing is yours to give—your Kalis stick will always live."

I was starting to feel a little grouchy myself. "I'll get lost in Aventurine or risk being expelled forever before I'll part with my Kalis stick," I said. This actually seemed to be the right tone for the elf.

"So wise are you, and honorable, too." The elf paused, rubbing his pointy chin as he considered our dilemma. "No trade means I cannot tell you which path to take, but I'll give a hint for a favor's sake."

"So if I do you a favor, we're even?" I asked.

The elf nodded. "Take a message to my brother, then nothing more will we owe one another."

"And how will I find him?" I could not agree to anything that would take time or divert me from my quest.

"He'll find you if your path be true," the elf answered.

"Then I agree," I said.

The elf motioned for me to come closer. When I leaned down, he said quietly, as if someone might be listening, "Tell him that if the wind goes free, so will we."

"That's easy enough to remember," I said.

Then the elf kept his word and gave me the hint. He pointed to the mountain on the left and said, "Hourling for grace." Then he pointed to the middle mountain and said, "Dayling for the brave." He pointed to the last mountain. "Yearling for the serene." He dropped his arm. "Only one will save your place in Aventurine."

I laughed; this was a good hint for me. I was certain I knew what it meant. The Kalis sticks my mother gave my sisters and me each had a letter carved into them, but the letters didn't match our names. Aiti had said only: *You will know why when the time is right.* The time was right now—my stick was carved with a *D*. "I'll take the path to Dayling," I said.

"And the message, too. Don't forget, will you?" asked the elf.

"I won't forget," I assured him.

The little man leapt into the air and clapped his hands. He was gone in a flash, laughing as he bounded toward the boulders.

A thunderous rumbling and grating sound shook the ground. The stone wall was separating, making a space I could slip through. I didn't know how long it would stay that way, so I slung the coat over my shoulder and ran, blood pounding in my ears and my boots pounding on the sand.

When I was six feet from the opening, the wall had stopped moving. The opening was barely wide enough for me to squeeze through sideways. With rock pressing me front and back, I sucked my breath in as I forced my way through. My coat dragged on the ground, and the hem caught on something I couldn't see. I tugged, then pulled, to free it while I kept squeezing through the narrow opening. I pushed so hard to clear the stones that I landed in a bramble of berries when I fell through the gap.

The two halves of the wall slammed together behind me.

I stared at the towering wall with a strange sense of calm. I was out of breath and I was scraped and scratched, but I had survived. My mother had carved a *D* on my Kalis stick. She must have known I would be making this journey.

Biba's voice and my destiny lay ahead—on the mountain called Dayling.